THE LAST VOYAGE
OF THE STEAMER
BARNARD CLINTON

Other Books by David E. Unruh

The Missouri River Murders
Train to Cheyenne

THE LAST VOYAGE
OF THE STEAMER
BARNARD CLINTON

•

David E. Unruh

AVALON BOOKS
NEW YORK

Published by Avalon Books,
an imprint of Thomas Bouregy & Co., Inc.
New York, NY

Library of Congress Cataloging-in-Publication Data

Unruh, David.
   The last voyage of the steamer Barnard Clinton / David E. Unruh.
       p. cm.
   ISBN 978-0-8034-7401-7 (hardcover : acid-free paper)
1. Steamboats—Fiction.   2. Missouri River—Fiction.   I. Title.
PS3621.N67L37 2012
813'.6—dc23

                                        2011039997

PRINTED IN THE UNITED STATES OF AMERICA
ON ACID-FREE PAPER
BY RR DONNELLEY, HARRISONBURG, VIRGINIA

To my wife, Carol, for her patience and love

Prologue

I saw it with my own eyes, sir!" the lieutenant told the major.

"Our doctor . . . treating a wounded Confederate . . . before seeing to our own wounded?" The major repeated what he had been told.

"Yes!" The lieutenant threw his chest out to show his anger at the memory of what he had seen earlier that day.

"There were no other medical people in attendance?" the major asked slowly. Seated at his folding table, he could look out over the field near Five Forks and see the bodies of both Union and Confederate soldiers, still lying where they had fallen. Weary men in blue uniforms were making their way through the field, arranging the bodies for pickup by wagons. There were no hearses available.

"No, sir."

"How many wounded were in the tent?"

"Seventeen."

"Could you tell the nature of their wounds?"

"Bad," was all the lieutenant would say.

The major avoided the opportunity for sarcasm. *Were there any good wounds?* he thought. "Were any of these men still on their feet?"

"Well, yes, I guess some were," the lieutenant replied.

"Did all of them survive the day?"

The lieutenant looked at his feet before answering. This

wasn't going the way he had wanted it to go. "I'm not sure," he lied. It had been a fierce battle. Many on both sides had perished, but the aid tent in question had been designated for noncritical casualties. The severely wounded Confederate had arrived there as an act of mercy on the part of some unidentified litter bearers.

"Did the wounded Southern officer survive?"

"If he did, it was only because that doctor ignored the bleeding of our own men!" the lieutenant exclaimed.

"But you don't know? Never mind, that's not the issue."

"There were others who saw the same thing I saw, Major!"

The major knew that this lieutenant had spent most of the war out of the action and might be now looking to make his mark before it was too late. "Very well, Lieutenant. Where is the doctor now?"

"She left in a carriage."

"She?"

"Yes, sir, she just went down the line of our men and then—"

The major interrupted. "This doctor was a woman?"

"Yes, sir."

"Not an Army doctor, then?"

"No, sir."

The major made some notes on the paper in front of him, paused, and looked at the lieutenant for a few minutes before answering. "Take a detail of five men and bring her back here." He pulled his watch from his pocket to check the time. "We'll convene a hearing in the morning, whether or not she is present."

The major found nothing in the lieutenant's attitude to admire. As this had likely been the last major battle of the war, he couldn't see any reason to investigate the actions of a civilian that were inspired more by compassion than by politics. But the lieutenant was not likely to let the matter drop, and he didn't want his actions reviewed later.

"I'll bring the traitoress back, sir," the lieutenant said and saluted. He didn't wait for the major to return the salute but turned and strode rapidly away. The major waved as if swatting a fly and returned to his notes.

Chapter One

May 1866

Robert Pruitt silently cursed the fact that the *Barnard Clinton* was a sternwheeler and not a sidewheeler. The ferry going to East St. Louis had pinched him off against the western side of the Mississippi River. Rather than delay his turn, which would have put him downstream from his assigned berth, he had continued his turn, thinking, hoping, that the 230-foot-long steamer could turn in the remaining water between itself and the steamers tied up at the wharf. This was only his third week as a certified pilot, his first arrival at St. Louis, and it looked as if his career might acquire an early blemish.

Steamers always berthed at an upstream angle. If approaching from upstream, one had to make a wide turn and finish with the bow pointed into the berth, coasting in as the speed bled off, arriving at the bank as the boat lost all its way. This had been Pruitt's strategy until the East St. Louis ferry crossed in front of him.

His options were to either take evasive action and end up hundreds of yards downstream or try to salvage his original approach. He had chosen the latter.

If he had been piloting a sidewheeler, he could have reversed one wheel and spun around in his own wake. He had done this many times during his apprenticeship on a sidewheeler. Sternwheelers, however, were not as maneuverable as sidewheelers, and the *Clinton* was in danger of plowing right through the line of steamers tied up at St. Louis. He could still use his engines in concert, though, so he rang for full astern as he approached the berth that the wharfmaster had indicated to him. He spun the big wheel rapidly to larboard, as he heard the engines stop. Now the safety of the steamer was in the hands of the engineer.

In the engine room the engineer was also cursing, loudly. It was not a simple manner to reverse the driving wheel on a steamboat. The steam had to be stopped and bypassed with large, heavy valves; a heavy rod had to be lifted out of its notch and placed in another notch, which reversed the timing of the inlet valves. Then the main valve had to be opened to the engine. And this had to be done in a well-coordinated manner with the two engines. The exasperated engineer performed the tasks on the larboard engine while his striker followed his motions exactly on the starboard engine.

As the stern wheel started turning in reverse, the bow of the *Clinton*, only two boat lengths from the line of steamers at the wharf, slowed. The rudders, located between the wheel and the stern, and in the powerful reverse flow of water, forced the stern downriver. Pruitt rang for half ahead and spun the wheel to starboard. The engineer and striker, with energy fueled by anger, reversed the tasks they had just completed.

The current carried the *Clinton* down until she was exactly opposite her assigned berth, and the bow lined up perfectly. Pruitt rang for slow ahead then stop, and the big steamer slid into her berth and touched the bottom gently. It would have been a masterful performance were it not for the perspiration on Pruitt's face.

Captain Culpepper spent most of his waking time in the pilot-house, but spoke only on rare occasions. This was one of those. "Will that be your customary manner of berthing this vessel?"

The Previous Year in a Conference Room,
Somewhere in Boston

"What do you think will be your biggest problem?" the banker asked the investor.

"Indians. The weather."

"No. Your biggest problem will be the river. Anybody with a saw can put together a flatboat and bring freight down the river. A railroad can't compete with a flatboat."

"They can have their buffalo hides. We'll make money taking goods to the frontier."

"There are plenty of steamboats going upriver and freighters waiting for loads. They'll take the cream off the top."

"I think the days of the steamboats are coming to an end."

"It would be better if they came to an end soon," the banker said. He watched the investor's face to make sure his comment was not taken lightly. Then he signed the document in front of him.

An Office Somewhere in Omaha, 1866

"You can start laying track next month," the investor told his company president. "The right of way to Fort Buford is soon to be forthcoming."

"That's the part of the river that the big steamboats are navigating," the president said. "Wouldn't it be better to start laying tracks from there west?"

"No. I want to compete directly with those big steamboats and show the world that rail is the future of transportation in the West. We *must* get a rail across the northern plains."

"The *Barnard Clinton* reached Fort Benton with few problems. Everyone's talking about it; more riverboat operators are coming west. And the transcontinental track is behind schedule."

"I've heard about the *Barnard Clinton*. If you want to have a profitable railroad, you should hope the *Clinton* doesn't make her second trip."

"Hope never filled anyone's bank account."

The investor's eyes narrowed. "Then do more than hope," he said slowly.

Captain Culpepper addressed his assembled group of officers. "Gentlemen, in spite of a few difficulties, we have had a successful trip. We have an opportunity, because of our early return to St. Louis and the blessings of a higher than average amount of snow in the Rocky Mountains, to repeat that trip this year if we act with dispatch."

The men nodded their approval. The senior officers—pilots, mates, engineers, purser—had all received bonuses based on the profits of the first trip.

"Several of you are leaving us, and you take with you my gratitude for your performance and a recommendation to your next employer."

The men looked around at one another.

"Mr. Singletary, the senior pilot, has already left; Mr. Pruitt will be the junior pilot and Mr. Felden will become the senior pilot." The captain nodded at Felden, then continued. "Our purser, Mr. James, is leaving as soon as I can secure a replacement."

Several men started to offer James their hand, but the captain's authoritarian voice discouraged them as he continued.

"The U.S. Army has contracted with the *Barnard Clinton* to deliver two hundred fifty-seven tons of freight as far up the Missouri as can be navigated. We will spend the next two days loading this and other freight, and loading passengers. Work hours for *all* hands will be from first to last light until we cast off."

One of the engineers raised his hand to speak.

"Yes, Mr. Van Dusen?"

"I didn't like the way we approached our berth . . . Captain," he said as he looked directly at Robert Pruitt. He never would have challenged Greg Singletary or Charles Felden this way, but he hadn't taken to young Pruitt in the few weeks he had worked with him, and he believed that Pruitt was not up to the task of piloting a sternwheeler on the Missouri River.

The captain knew exactly what was bothering Peter Van Dusen, but the steamer was not a democracy. "The pilot on duty will operate the vessel according to river rules, experience, and common sense. Your duty is to respond to the engine room telegraph promptly every time," the captain said sternly, looking around the room. "Are there any other questions?"

A Hotel Room in St. Louis, 1866

"Let the boat get far enough upstream that help won't be available," the company president told the man. "And no witnesses."

"Past Omaha?"

"Yes, but not too far past. We'll want the story in the Omaha news. And early failure is to our advantage."

"People might get hurt."

"Yes."

"Or killed."

"The more risk that's demonstrated, the better."

"If I blow the boilers, it might kill everyone."

The company president didn't acknowledge that shocking statement. He only said, "Find someone reliable to help you."

"All right. I'm going down there now to have an interview with the captain."

"Don't come back here."

Chapter Two

Five years in hotels, two years on the Mississippi River?" It really wasn't a question to which Captain Culpepper expected a reply, but the man answered.

"Yes, sir."

"What did you do during the war?"

"I managed transient officers' quarters in Washington, D.C."

"Rank?"

"I was a civilian under contract."

"Many of our practices onboard the *Barnard Clinton* are military in nature," Captain Culpepper said. "You'll be expected to understand."

"That presents no problem," the new purser replied.

"Very well, Mr. Galloway. The purser's office is on the boiler deck in the main salon. The present purser's name is Mr. James. Find him, and as soon as he has given you an understanding of his duties, send him to me. You will start your duties immediately."

"Yes, sir." Galloway started to salute as he had seen Army personnel do, but the captain had turned his attention to papers on his desk. Galloway realized the interview was over and, looking back over his shoulder once, left the captain's room to follow his instructions.

Danny Barton, the security officer on the *Barnard Clinton*, turned his back as the captain opened the safe in his room, then turned to watch as he removed twelve sturdy haversacks, each weighing more than thirty pounds, and laid them on his desk and the top of the safe. He closed the safe.

"When Mr. James arrives, you and he will take this gold into town. I'll go with you long enough to sign the papers at the bank."

"Yes, sir," Barton said, then added, "I'm going to get Weedeater to accompany us with a rifle."

"Very well."

Barton left to find the roustabout known as Weedeater. Weedeater had proven his worth with a rifle on the voyage that had just ended, and Danny had come to rely on him.

Fifteen minutes later, Danny, the captain, the purser, and Weedeater walked off the *Barnard Clinton*, hired a hack, and rode into St. Louis. The purser, James, broke the silence as the hack left the waterfront and rattled its way into town.

"As soon as we deliver the gold, Captain, with your permission, I'll be leaving you. I have train tickets to Baltimore on a train leaving tomorrow, and I want to catch the next ferry to East St. Louis."

"Very well, Mr. James. I wish you good fortune. You served us well."

"I hope Mr. Galloway serves you to your satisfaction."

"Is there doubt in your mind?" The captain's question did not express surprise.

"Yes."

The captain apparently did not intend to explore the subject further, trusting his own judgment more than the purser's, but Danny did.

"What should we watch for, Mr. James?" he asked. The captain's face showed no change.

"I don't know." The purser was thoughtful for a moment. He had taken an instant dislike to his replacement, unusual for a man who was skilled and enjoyed dealing with people of all sorts. "His fingernails were dirty." James was fastidious in his personal appearance. "Although we are the same size, he expressed displeasure at having to wear my uniform coat."

Danny, who had leaned forward in his seat, now leaned back. These complaints did not seem serious to him, but what James said next renewed his interest in the new purser.

"He had a large revolver, which he put into his desk drawer, and he put a pocket revolver into his inside coat pocket."

Pursers handled some money, although not in great amounts. James had never been armed, but it could be that the new purser was merely taking precautions in case of trouble. Or it could be he was himself trouble.

The captain had listened to James but still offered no comment. Danny started to say something and then thought better of it. After all, most of the men onboard the *Barnard Clinton* carried some sort of weapon. The male passengers often wore sidearms or carried long guns; the roustabouts all carried large knives. The officers, alone, with the exception of Danny Barton, were unarmed, but there was no vessel regulation that prohibited them from being armed, and both pilots had keys to the cabinet that held the vessel's rifles and ammunition. Galloway's actions seemed unusual but not threatening.

Due to congestion on the street where the bank was located, the hack was not able to deliver the men to the front door. It was forced to stop about one hundred yards east of the bank, so the four men got out. The captain told the driver to come up and wait when he was able, and they began walking, Danny in front, carrying two of the haversacks, and the captain and James each carrying three haversacks. Weedeater stayed at the hack to guard the other four sacks. It was obvious to all on the street what was in the sacks.

On the second trip the captain and the purser carried the sacks while Danny led the way and Weedeater brought up the rear. Four tough-looking men had taken up position on the boardwalk and stood as a human barricade between the *Barnard Clinton*'s men and the bank. Danny stopped short as it became obvious that they would not give way.

The boardwalk was not narrow; there was more than enough room for the two groups of men to pass each other, but the four toughs didn't budge. They shifted their weight back and forth slightly as a subtle warning that they were digging into their position.

Danny tried a disarming smile. "How about giving us room to pass, fellows?"

One of the men smirked and snorted. No one moved.

Captain Culpepper hefted his two haversacks higher on his shoulder, flaunting their weight and leaving no doubt as to their contents. Then he stepped around Danny, saying, "Mr. Barton, I'm going through these men to the bank. Kill the first one who touches his gun."

Danny and the captain had served together during the last year of the Civil War, and Danny had followed the captain, a colonel then, on many a charge. He stepped in behind the captain and watched the two men on the right side of the group closely. James, although anxious, followed Danny. Weedeater, seeing Danny watching the two men to the right, kept his eyes on the two to the left.

The four men gave way to the advance. Maybe it was the way Danny wore his revolver, not in a cavalry holster but in a cutdown holster, that gave quick access; maybe it was the fact that although the men looked tough, none looked rougher or tougher than Weedeater, and he was carrying a repeating rifle. But the real reason was the look in the captain's eyes that told the four men he cared nothing for their lives if they interfered with him. As the crew passed, Weedeater turned and walked backward while he watched the four who had lost all their belligerence. They had asserted themselves and failed, and they only wanted to get away in hopes that everyone who had seen them forgot the incident soon.

At the bank the gold was carefully weighed and then taken away. The bank gave Captain Culpepper some cash, deposited a portion of his credit into his business account, and gave him a letter of credit to take with him upriver. He shook the banker's hand and then joined Danny, James, and Weedeater on the boardwalk outside. The hack had found its way through the congestion and was waiting.

"We'll take you to the ferry landing, Mr. James," the captain offered.

Chapter Three

Galloway found a roustabout lounging on the cargo deck. "Come with me," he said. The man, noting Galloway's officer's uniform, followed him to the main cabin where the purser's office was located.

Galloway indicated a portable writing table. "Take this table to the front of the boat where the passengers come onboard. And this chair also."

"You mean the bow?" the roustabout asked with contempt.

"Yes, of course!" Galloway gave him a look that expressed his own contempt for the shabbily dressed man.

Without further comment the man stacked the chair on the table and lifted them both, following Galloway to the main stairs.

The stages were well-constructed gangplanks that most steamers carried on the bow. Upon tying up, the stages were lowered into place with ropes. They were sturdy enough that livestock and wagons could be driven across them. Sometimes, on low landings, they sloped downward from the bow of the steamer; most of the time they sloped upward to the bank, or as in this case, to a purpose-built wharf.

Galloway directed the roustabout to set up the table at the boat end of the larboard stage and then he spread his registry, his inkpot, cashbox, and various forms and paperwork on it. The starboard stage was being used to load cargo; there was a small group of people waiting on the landing next to the larboard stage. Galloway motioned for them to come aboard and upon his signal several men stepped aside for an attractive woman dressed in the high style of the day. She stepped gracefully onto the stage and walked slowly down to the bow of the steamer. Galloway rushed to the end of the stage to take her hand as she stepped onto the deck. Her perfume drifted across the bow like the smell of a blooming orchard on a spring breeze. Work stopped.

"I have reservations for a private cabin," she said, as if she expected that would explain everything.

"May I know your name, please?" Galloway asked, as he sat down again behind his table.

"Oh, of course. My name is Abigail Demille." Her voice was soft yet clear, and carried well. Everyone within a hundred yards had waited to see if they could hear her identify herself, and they weren't disappointed.

"Yes, Miss Demille, your room is already paid. Here is your key. There's a menu in your cabin. Do you have trunks?"

"Oh, my, yes. There are five in all. The hotel is sending them over."

"Would you like help with your grip?" She was carrying a black leather satchel that, although expensive looking, didn't seem to match her stylish dress.

"No, I can manage it quite well," she answered, and then added, "How nice of you to ask."

"All right, then." Galloway smiled what he thought was his best smile. "Enjoy your trip on the *Barnard Clinton*."

"I'm sure I will. Thank you, Mr. . . . ?" She leaned forward with raised eyebrows.

"Galloway. Jack Galloway." He tried to improve his smile even more. She curtsied her thanks and briefly touched his arm as she left to follow the roustabout to her room. His eyes followed her across the bow and up the main stairs. Then he turned and stiffened himself to his business.

"Next!"

Many of the passengers were poor immigrants who had sold everything to afford passage to the frontier. Galloway treated them differently than he had treated Abigail Demille.

"You must sleep in the cargo bay. Do not build any fires, don't disturb the freight," Galloway lectured the poorly dressed man with some relish. "Do not go up to the boiler deck except when notified at mealtime. You eat only at third call. Your meals are twenty cents. You are not allowed to take food out of the dining room. Do not go to the third deck for any reason. Do you understand?"

"Yes."

"Any infraction of these rules will result in your being put off the boat immediately."

The man lifted the heavy bag that contained all his possessions and stepped away to find a place in the cargo bay where he would spend the next many weeks.

"Next."

A tall man wearing a pistol belt and carrying a rifle and a satchel stepped forward. His clothes were expensive but well worn, as was the satchel. "Main cabin," the man said.

"Name?"

"Harvey Blake."

"Destination?"

"Fort Benton."

"One hundred eighty dollars."

Harvey Blake removed a letter from his pocket and smoothed it onto the table in front of Galloway. "This is a travel voucher from the stockholders."

Galloway smirked. He recognized the document, but he only said, "Very well. You have berth seventeen on the right side. The starboard side."

"There aren't any staterooms on the main deck?"

"No."

"I wanted a private room."

Galloway met the man's stare. "They're on the Texas deck, and they're all spoken for."

Blake gave Galloway an ugly look and then strode to the main stairway.

"Next!" Galloway shouted.

So it went for several hours. As passengers would show up at the boarding stage, Galloway would register them, give them the briefest of instructions, and wait for the next one or the next group. Army officers had private staterooms, two to a room; noncommissioned officers had berths in the main cabin, beds in two tiers along both walls of the dining room, separated from the room by individual curtains. Unaccompanied women and women with female children shared one large cabin at the aft end of the main cabin, separated by a heavy curtain that was drawn from wall to wall at nine P.M. every evening. Enlisted men carried bedrolls and made their own beds in the cargo bay or on the bow wherever they could find room. They shared the space with other deck passengers and all the roustabouts.

When Galloway had filled all the available berths, he placed a barricade across the larboard stage with a small sign that said NO MORE PASSENGERS. Then he carried the paperwork and money back up to his office. The bartenders and the kitchen staff were his responsibility. He toured the kitchen and the bar, not sure of himself but wanting to know that everything was in order now that the passengers were aboard. Soon they would be ordering food and drink.

Later that evening the last of the cargo was loaded, and the first mate, Steve Allenby, climbed to the pilothouse.

"Captain, we're all loaded. We're a little beyond our marks, but we'll unload eighty tons at Omaha." Allenby passed his paperwork to the captain, who tucked it under his arm.

"Very well, Mr. Allenby. We'll have an officer's meeting as soon as they can be assembled in my stateroom. See to that."

"Yes, sir," Allenby replied and left the pilothouse to inform the other officers. The captain left to go to his room.

Ten minutes later seven officers and Danny Barton were gathered outside the captain's cabin. He opened the door and beckoned them in. The captain's cabin was scarcely large enough to hold nine men, but they knew they would not be there long. The captain was not wordy.

"Gentlemen, most of you have met Robert Pruitt, who will be taking Greg Singletary's place. Our new purser is Jack Galloway. He comes with good references. Give him any assistance he requests." He looked around. "Based on the last three years, we can surmise that there will be relatively high water through the end of July. We'll try to reach Fort Benton again this year. We'll be traveling day and night until we get beyond Omaha, and then night travel will depend on weather, moonlight, and, of course, the pilot."

The captain paused. No one commented, and he continued.

"We'll resume standing regular Navy watches beginning now. A-watch will finish this evening's watch; B-watch will take over at midnight. Mr. Allenby, give us a report on cargo."

"We have cannonballs and twenty barrels of gunpowder in the hold, along with sixty tons of rails, rail spikes, and thirty-two barrels of whiskey. In the cargo bay we have flour in barrels, coffee, housewares belonging to some of the passengers, six horses, and eleven cows. Oh, and somewhere underneath the miscellaneous freight are four wagons and one Concord stagecoach."

"Very well. How about passengers?"

The purser stepped forward. "We have four Army officers, twenty-six enlisted men, ten male civilians, six women, and fifteen children. There are two firemen, sixteen roustabouts, ten kitchen staff, and four maids. There will be one hundred and two souls onboard to begin the voyage."

The purser shuffled his papers and then continued.

"The captain has the Texas cabin, the pilots share the Iowa cabin, the mates share the Ohio cabin, and the engineers share the Illinois cabin." He paused, raised his eyebrows, and then went on. "Mr. Barton has the Minnesota cabin, Mr. and Mrs. Willis have the Vermont cabin, Mrs. Link and her two daughters have the New York cabin, and Miss Demille has the Pennsylvania cabin. Four officers have the Delaware and Rhode Island cabins, the rest of the men will sleep in the men's cabin forward, and the three remaining women will sleep in the ladies' cabin aft, as will the maids. The ordinary roustabouts and deck passengers will sleep on deck. I understand I am to sleep in my office off the main salon."

"Thank you, Mr. Galloway. Give me the cash you collected and make me a copy of the passenger manifest before we get under way."

"Yes, sir," Galloway answered.

"Engineering?" The captain looked at William Brown, the senior engineer.

"We have forty-two cords of wood, all four boilers are on line, one hundred forty pounds of steam."

"Very well. I have informed the wharfmaster that we will be backing out at nine P.M. That gives us twenty minutes. Mr. Felden, report to the pilothouse and prepare to cast off."

"Yes, sir."

The captain didn't need to formally dismiss the men. They filed out and headed for their respective tasks. He followed Felden to the pilothouse.

In the pilothouse, the captain and the senior pilot were alone.

"Mr. Felden, we should be into the Missouri River before the change of watch."

"Yes, sir."

"If that turns out not to be the case, wake me and remain in the pilothouse with Mr. Pruitt."

Felden hoped he didn't understand. If the captain didn't

have confidence in Robert Pruitt, he should say it right out. The mouth of the Missouri was not the easiest entrance, but it was marked. And although Pruitt was newly certified, the examination for pilots was comprehensive. It wasn't an easy thing to gain certification as a Missouri River pilot. If he questioned the captain further, though, it would be the first time since hiring on that he would do so.

"Yes, sir," was his reply.

While this was happening, Danny Barton was prowling every corner of the boat. He walked along both sides of the stateroom deck, called the Texas deck, where most of the staterooms had their doors open wide. The passengers were staying awake to watch the departure from St. Louis. He spoke with each of them briefly, particularly the beautiful Miss Abigail Demille, about whom everyone was curious. He learned nothing, because she was more adept at extracting information than he was. After a few minutes of pleasant conversation he descended to the main salon, the so-called boiler deck. The curtain across the ladies cabin had been drawn, and some of the individual berths also had their curtains drawn. Most passengers, however, were also anticipating the departure, and in the meantime, there were a few quiet card games in progress.

Barton next descended to the main, or cargo, deck. The roustabouts were lifting the stages one at a time with the help of a capstan driven by the doctor engine. A spindle shaped like a reverse barrel, the capstan was located in the center of the bow, where it could be used to do a variety of tasks. By wrapping a line around it as it turned, a huge load could be moved just by keeping tension around the spindle. It was dangerous work, however. If a roustabout were to get caught between the incoming line and the capstan, he would be crushed by the rope as it wound around the spindle. If there were not enough turns to bind the rope to the spindle, as when the load was very heavy, the roustabout would have to put another loop over the spindle, and the line would try to back up as the load temporarily overpowered the friction between it and the turning metal. The roustabout handling the line had to be very quick and strong, and this one was. In minutes the larboard stage was raised and tied off, and the crew began rigging the starboard stage for raising.

The doctor engine was a recent improvement on riverboats. It could turn the capstan, power the bilge pump, power the boiler feed water pump, or power the firefighting pump. Prior to its introduction, steamers could take on water only when under way. The addition of a small steam engine cured this problem and others, and thus was nicknamed the doctor engine.

Barton walked into the cargo bay where more roustabouts were stowing freight. Preparations for departure had been so hurried that freight and cordwood were intermingled. Steve Allenby knew the captain would not be pleased if he failed to check the cargo bay before departure, and he was exhorting the men to make the cargo bay presentable.

"Hey! You!" Allenby shouted at a roustabout. "There's no sense putting Omaha freight underneath freight for Fort Union."

"He cain't read, mate," another roustabout explained.

"Then show him what to do!"

"I cain't read neither," the man said.

Allenby calmed down a little. He faced the man squarely and lowered his voice to a near-normal level.

"What's your name, mister?"

"Frog."

"All right, Frog, find someone who can read and start stowing this freight so you don't have to do a whole day's work just to get it unloaded."

"All right, mate."

Allenby noticed Barton watching and just shook his head as he made his way through the freight to direct some other roustabouts. Barton smiled and continued past the boilers deeper into the cargo bay where the livestock was stabled. He had learned a lot from the hostler who had taken care of a large herd of horses on the first trip. He noted with satisfaction that the corrals were built to the pattern that the previous hostler had established.

Near the aft end of the cargo bay was the engine room. William Brown and his striker had made all the preparations necessary for backing away from the wharf. All that was necessary was to respond to the engine room telegraph. Barton checked his watch; it was five minutes before nine P.M.

"How are you this evening, Will?" Danny asked.

"Anxious to get moving so we get some fresh air through here," he answered. It was a warm St. Louis night, and the heat from the boilers and steam lines had made the engine room and the entire cargo bay warm.

"It should be any minute. The larboard stage is up, and the starboard stage should be almost there."

At that moment a roustabout came into the engine room and gestured to Brown to shut the doctor engine down. Danny knew the signal from the pilothouse for reverse power would come at any second, and he left the engine room through the back door, which exited onto the lower walkway.

As he made his way forward, he had a clear view of the bow and the wharf beyond. If the departure had been during daylight hours, there probably would have been a brass band on the wharf. In spite of the late hour, there was a small crowd of relatives and well-wishers watching in anticipation.

At that moment the whistle blew a long blast, and the sternwheel began turning in reverse. A cheer went up from the crowd as the dockhands threw the lines over to the roustabouts on the bow, and the vessel slowly made its way out of its berth. They continued cheering as the boat, with every lamp lit, gained the middle of the river, blew its whistle again, and started forward. The SS *Barnard Clinton* began its second voyage of 1866.

Chapter Four

The *Clinton*'s departure from St. Louis was much less dramatic than the arrival. As Charles Felden gathered sternway out of the *Clinton*'s berth, he looked around and saw he had the wide Mississippi to himself. He rang for stop, and the engines quit puffing, but the steamer coasted out to the middle of the river, the wheel lazily turning in reverse from the force of water against it.

Down below, William Brown, anticipating that Felden would let the *Clinton* coast, did not apply the brakes to the wheel immediately. Then, as if reading Felden's mind, he stopped the wheel, and he and the striker changed the rods that controlled the inlet valve timing, and then he waited. His actions were right on time. In a matter of seconds Felden rang for half ahead, and Brown slowly opened the main steam valve as his striker released the brake. The pitman arm on the right side pushed for ninety degrees, and then the arm on the left side took over for ninety degrees. At the end of that arc, the pitman arm on the right side pulled, followed ninety degrees later by the arm on the left. The engine room, which had been quiet and still for the days in port, was now alive. The pitman arms drove out and in, the valve linkages clattered, steam whistled through the pipes, and the engines huffed at ten strokes per minute, two huffs for each revolution, forty hissing moans per minute. Felden rang for full ahead, and the wheel slowly gained from ten revolutions per minute to twenty as the floating hotel came up to full speed.

The *Barnard Clinton*'s construction and layout was similar to many other Missouri River steamers. The hull was five and a half feet deep and decked over full length. Built onto the deck was the cargo bay, which had a twelve-foot ceiling. The first thirty feet at the bow was uncovered. Forward in the cargo bay were the boilers and fireboxes, situated to balance the weight of the engines and stern wheel aft. On top of the cargo bay was the main cabin, housing from front to back the bar and kitchen, the dining area with berths on both sides, and then the ladies' cabin. The kitchen was actually located on the forward starboard side, and the bar, storeroom, and purser's office were located opposite, leaving a wide space in the center where dining passengers could access the main stairway going down to the bow. On top of the main cabin (known traditionally as the boiler deck) was the pilothouse, raised four feet above the staterooms and the bathhouse. Beyond the bathhouse, there were the uppermost, uncovered structures known as the hurricane deck, the aft end of which looked down on the stern wheel. Like most Missouri River steamers, there was a minimum of luxury furnishings. In comparison to other Missouri River steamers, however, the *Clinton* was broader of beam and shallower of hull, with a minimum of superstructure to catch the prairie winds.

Danny Barton had traveled from the staterooms to the main cabin to the cargo bay to the hold, and now he was back on the hurricane deck, walking past the staterooms and climbing the short staircase to the pilothouse.

Felden glanced around as Barton entered the pilothouse.

"Mr. Barton," he said as he returned his attention to the river, "did you find everything in order?"

"Yes. With all the Army personnel onboard, we might have a less eventful trip this time, don't you agree?"

"One can hope, but don't take anything for granted."

"No. And no matter what we think of our passengers,

we'll have many dealings with people about which we know nothing."

"I prefer to deal with the river. She never pretends to be something she's not."

"I wish I understood people the way you understand the river."

Felden snorted a grin as a means to acknowledge the compliment modestly and then redirected the conversation.

"Have you any suspicions about any of our passengers?" Before Barton could answer, he continued. "Be quiet for a few moments. We're nearing the mouth of the Missouri."

Danny complied and for the next half hour, Felden maneuvered in confusing currents and eddies and then was in the Missouri. Down below, the engineer was ready to make adjustments to speed, but he doubted that Felden would need anything, and he was right.

"Mr. Barton, we are now in the Missouri River," Felden announced.

Danny picked up the conversation where they had left off. "I am curious about one of the passengers . . . a woman," he said.

Felden knew Danny enough to know that his interest was professional and said nothing.

Danny continued. "She presents such a dramatic appearance that I could draw some conclusions about her lifestyle, but something tells me she is truly a lady."

Felden nodded. He had seen the lady and had come to the same conclusion. "You're referring to Miss Demille, no doubt."

"Yes," Danny replied. "You remember the lady on the last voyage, how much trouble centered around her."

"Yes."

"Miss Demille reminds me of her in many ways. The kind of woman who makes men do things they might not otherwise do. Does that make sense?"

"Yes," Felden smiled. "Well put, young man. But if she is

your only problem, we're way ahead of where we were on the last trip."

"That's true. There are a couple of men who will bear watching, but that's all."

"We'll be fine if we can keep water out of the boat and the boat off the sand," Felden said.

Danny thought about what he wanted to say next for a few moments. He wasn't sure it was a proper topic of conversation—almost like gossip. Felden kept quiet, knowing Barton was struggling with something.

Danny finally spoke. "Is Pruitt a good replacement for Singletary?"

"Singletary has made more trips on the Missouri than anyone except perhaps Joseph LaBarge. A good pilot never stops learning. Pruitt has a lot to learn. He's about your age, isn't he?"

"Younger, I think."

"He'll make mistakes, but if he's made right, he'll learn from them. And, besides, I'll never be more than two hundred feet away."

Danny knew it would take an incredibly bad situation for Felden to interfere with another pilot, but he nevertheless took some comfort from Felden's defense of Pruitt.

There was a tap on the pilothouse door and the topic of conversation, Robert Pruitt, entered, followed by the second mate and the B-watch engineer. The change of watch was imminent.

Pruitt examined the chart and compared it with what he could see of the shoreline. There were still occasional lights in habitations, and the skyline was visible against the dark blue starry sky.

"We must be opposite Hamilton's barns right now, Mr. Felden?"

Felden managed a quick smile for Danny as he answered. "Exactly so."

Pruitt stood up from the chart table and was silent. The first mate and the A-watch engineer entered the pilothouse.

"The stern wheel is a little lumpy, Mr. Van Dusen," Brown said. "We'll investigate at daylight. It probably picked up some driftwood. We'll be on watch at daylight, and we'll find out. Other than that, everything is in order." Van Dusen nodded.

The first mate, Steve Allenby, spoke. "I found a barrel of gunpowder that never made it to the hold. I pushed it into the corral to keep it away from the deckers' cook fires. We'll get it into the hold come morning. Other than that, the roustabouts did a good job of stowing the freight."

"All right," Erickson said. "Thanks, Steve."

There was some small talk until, as the second hand of the pilothouse clock lined up with the other two hands, Felden rang the bell eight times. The A-watch retired to their bunks and the B-watch officers set themselves to their tasks. Barton stayed in the pilothouse to talk to Pruitt.

Pruitt was tall and thin, which contributed to his youthful appearance. His mass of blond hair was uncombed, but his face showed no trace of a beard, leading Danny to speculate that he didn't yet shave, but in fact he did. Pruitt had been a replacement pilot when Greg Singletary, the B-watch pilot, fell ill and left the *Clinton*. Upstream from Omaha, the *Clinton* usually stopped at night, allowing Felden, as the only pilot, some rest, but when she came back down, Captain Culpepper wanted the ability to travel at night and thus needed another pilot. Pruitt had been available at Council Bluffs, and the captain hired him.

"We haven't had a chance to talk since you came aboard, Mr. Pruitt. Would you mind some company for a while?"

"Not at all, Mr. Barton," Pruitt replied.

"There's usually some coffee left in the pot in the kitchen. Can I get you some?"

"Oh, boy," Pruitt said, "that would be very nice."

Barton left and returned in minutes with two cups of

lukewarm coffee. Pruitt was holding a watch in his hand and motioned for the security officer not to speak. He was counting to himself. Finally, he spoke.

"Thanks for the coffee, and thanks for not saying anything; I was counting revolutions."

"What does that tell you?"

"A lot of things. How the engines are running, how well the boilers are fired, if there's no wind, how fast we're going through the water." As he talked he brought the watch up and looked from it to a point of light in the distance. "Now I'm going to check our speed over the ground." He made a notation in his notebook.

"How do you do that?" Barton asked.

"We just passed another light that burns all night in someone's yard. In about thirty minutes we'll come abreast of a small island, and Felden has both landmarks noted on his chart. I'll calculate our speed over this known distance by using the time it takes to cover it." As he talked, Pruitt was never still. He went from side to side in the pilothouse, never taking one hand off the wheel as he watched the stars, the skyline, the faint reflections on the water, and the surface illuminated dimly by the *Clinton*'s lamps.

"Wouldn't the speed be the same every time?"

"That would be ideal, but it never happens."

Barton would have been impressed if not for the fact that he had never seen Felden do these things. Pruitt responded to his unspoken doubts.

"Pilots like Charles Felden and Greg Singletary have all this in their head. Felden has been a pilot all his life. I don't have their experience, so I make notes."

Now he was impressed. "I'm glad you're doing it and not me."

"I'm glad I don't need to wear a gun. How many times have you been shot at?"

"Since the war ended, not often."

"It takes only once, you know."

"I know," Barton said.

The two young men talked until the watch was half over. They had a lot in common, but it was the things that each found strange and interesting in the other that helped start a friendship. Barton reluctantly left just after two A.M. to get as much sleep as possible before daylight.

Chapter Five

Three nights later the *Clinton* was making steady progress against the current between Jefferson City, Missouri, and Providence. Robert Pruitt was at the helm and was maneuvering the big steamer through some swifter and shallower water. He examined the charts and his and Felden's notebooks frequently between times of spinning the wheel one direction and then the other and ringing for slower or faster engine speed. The changes in engine speed had awakened the captain, and he was now standing behind Pruitt in the pilothouse. He habitually did this when he heard the engines change note, no matter who the pilot happened to be at the time.

The Missouri River steamboat industry had been slow to adopt sternwheelers. Sidewheelers had worked well on the Mississippi and Ohio rivers for several decades, and pilots liked the better maneuverability. When builders began installing banks of rudders between the stern and the stern wheel, the agility gap was narrowed considerably, and the main advantage of the sternwheeler, protection of the wheel, was becoming the deciding factor on the more primitive and dangerous waters of the Missouri.

But Pruitt still wished he was piloting a sidewheeler. He became increasingly frustrated with the slow response of the *Clinton* and was spinning the wheel rapidly from lock to lock as the steamer yawed this way and that. Thanks to the bright moon and the quick response of the engineer in adjusting the speed of the engines, Pruitt had successfully navigated around several sandbars, avoided a snag, and now rang for full speed as the *Clinton* entered the main channel and encountered swifter water. The captain stood with his arms folded across his chest and said nothing.

Pruitt had another disadvantage. Whereas Charles Felden had much of the river committed to memory, Pruitt had neither the instincts nor the memory to enable him to safely navigate at night without occasional references to his notebook and the chart. He had a small oil lamp in a cubby hole under the chart table, which he had to retrieve to see the chart and then replace quickly so that he could watch the river.

Pruitt's frustration with the sternwheeler was in some ways understandable. His reliance on the chart and his notebook was acceptable, as was his routine for bringing the lamp to the table for improved vision. But in his anxiety, he had neglected an important method of navigating in strange waters.

Pruitt's second mate had taken it upon himself to put a roustabout on the bow with a lead line, and he diligently threw, retrieved the line, and called out the depth, but Pruitt, in his flurry of activity, was not paying heed. He could see indications of shallow water on the starboard side, and steadying the wheel with one hand, he leaned to the left to see the water ahead. The water was flat and smooth, often an indication of deep water, but in this case, unrecognized by Pruitt, an indication of calm, shallow water.

The pilothouse windows opened from the bottom. Pruitt was sweating and he quickly unlatched one of the windows and lifted it outward onto its strut. Then the whole situation revealed itself to him. He could see that what he thought was deep water was in fact shallow, and he could see and hear the leadsman on the bow shouting and waving. Then the bow of the

Clinton plowed into the shallow bottom. Her speed was such that the bow rode up onto the sandbar before she stopped, the forward fifty feet of the hull resting on the bottom.

Pruitt kicked at the stanchion that supported the wheel and swore under his breath. The captain, who had been silent and still until now, took one step forward, but before he could do anything else, Pruitt leaned out of the window and shouted to his second mate.

"Erickson, call all hands!"

"Yes, sir, Mr. Pruitt. Your engine telegraph must not be working." Erickson called back diplomatically, "Do you want me to have the engineer stop the engines?"

"Yes!" Pruitt cursed his lapse of judgment under his breath. "Then come to the pilothouse, please." In spite of Erickson's offer, Pruitt rang the engine room to stop the engines; obviously they anticipated the action, as the engines slowed their useless churning even as he operated the telegraph. It was 3:40 A.M.

Five minutes later, exactly fifteen minutes before the change of watch, Charles Felden entered the pilothouse. Pruitt and Erickson were conferring.

"The moon will be in the trees in ten minutes," Erickson pointed out. "We need to send a crew out in the yawl to find the channel while we have that light, and we should also sound the river downstream."

Felden said nothing. His first mate and engineer entered the pilothouse.

"I'd rather sound the river upstream and see if we can walk over this sandbar," said Pruitt. Erickson shrugged. The captain watched each man as the discussion went on.

"Mr. Felden," Pruitt said to the pilot coming on duty, "we'll try to have the *Clinton* afloat by eight bells."

Felden nodded slowly. He wasn't in agreement, but it would be ten minutes before he had responsibility for the vessel.

"Launch the yawl with a crew of five and plenty of lanterns,"

Pruitt ordered. "Have them find out what's ahead for a hundred yards, and then report back. We can send them downstream at that time, if it looks like it will be necessary."

Felden folded his arms and looked at his shoes. Erickson left the pilothouse to organize the yawl crew. There was an awkward silence in the pilothouse as the A-watch officers waited the last few minutes until they could take over. Pruitt studied the chart. As Erickson returned to the pilothouse to report that the yawl was in the water, Pruitt, noticing the second hand had just passed twelve, rang the bell eight times.

"Mr. Felden, she's yours, and she's in a sad state," Pruitt said, stating the obvious. "If you don't mind, I'd like to stand by here to observe and help if I can."

"I appreciate that, Mr. Pruitt," Felden said, stepping forward to the wheel. "Mr. Allenby, when the yawl gets back, tie it off and have the crew come back onboard. We'll do no further exploration until daylight."

"Very well," Allenby answered.

"Mr. Brown, we're down by the stern. When you get to the engine room, remove the hatches and keep an eye on the hold. Mind the powder kegs that are stored there when you use your lanterns."

"All right, Mr. Felden," Brown answered.

"You can let the fires go down. It'll start getting light in an hour, and then we'll see what can be done."

Brown left the pilothouse to carry out his instructions. Felden felt badly for Pruitt and turned to him as he leaned against the wheel. There were thirty-five years of difference in their ages.

"Mr. Pruitt, is this your first grounding?"

"Yes," Pruitt answered through tight lips.

"It won't be your last." Felden had, himself, grounded many times. He didn't add that this grounding had been totally unnecessary, a result of Pruitt's lack of complete attention.

"I nevertheless do not look forward to the next one and shall make every effort to avoid it."

It was midafternoon before the *Clinton* was free of the sandbar. When the sun rose, the situation was more obvious, and the two pilots, changing watch every four hours, worked together according to the plan that Felden had formulated.

The submerged sandbar was found to extend hundreds of yards in front of the *Clinton*, and "grasshoppering," or walking, over it with gin poles was not realistic. A sounding at the stern revealed that there was almost eight feet of water depth there. Felden started the crew in shifting cargo to the stern as much as possible. Pruitt came back on duty at eight A.M. and continued moving cargo but also used four of the Army soldiers to take the yawl out and find the deep water that he had inadvertently steamed away from in the night.

At noon, Felden came on duty and ordered Brown to bring the boilers up. He set two anchors downstream and used the doctor engine to pull two lines tight. Then he instructed the engineer to slowly turn the wheel forward. This augmented the current flowing around the grounded bow. He put five roustabouts into the river on either side of the bow to shovel sand from around the bow into the current where it was carried away downstream. Opening up the area in the bar where the *Clinton* was stranded caused current to eat away at the bar, and soon there was slack appearing in the lines. The doctor engine was used again to pull the *Clinton* back, the roustabouts shoveled more sand, the stern wheel turned slowly forward, and before long the lines to the anchors were slack again.

Barton was in the pilothouse, watching the progress. "It looks like you're winning, Mr. Felden."

Felden answered as he watched the roustabouts in the water and the anchor lines being winched up. "What we don't know is where all the sand is going. We could be creating another sandbar behind us."

"How did Pruitt come to run aground?"

The captain was also in the pilothouse. Felden didn't want to criticize another pilot in his presence. He merely said, "It happens."

The captain cleared his throat. He also was reluctant to criticize one of his officers, but he and Felden were very close. "I'd be interested in your assessment, Mr. Felden."

Felden thought for a moment. "Pruitt does well when the river gets confusing. His eyesight is keen and his reflexes are quick. In this case, it might have been prudent to reduce speed a little, if only to make a grounding less severe." Felden was referring to how far the *Clinton* had plowed through the sand before stopping. "I usually open all the pilothouse windows at night to afford the clearest view of the water's surface and to better hear the leadsman."

Felden had to pause to step outside and shout instructions to two roustabouts handling the capstan that was taking up the anchor lines. They had let the line accumulate in a tangle beside the capstan.

"Gary! Little Bit! Coil that line properly!" They looked up and nodded. He added, "And quit standing in those bights unless you like the taste of Missouri River mud." They began attending to the line.

Felden reentered the pilothouse and continued. "Pruitt's real lapse was in not paying attention to his leadsman."

No one spoke for several minutes.

"Thank you, Mr. Felden," the captain said after the long pause. "That confirms my assessment."

Chapter Six

The next several days passed without incident. It was early summer, and the weather was on its best behavior: warm, still days that encouraged some passengers to gather next to the rail, and nights that could be tolerated with just a light jacket or a blanket while one sat in a deck chair and watched the sky turn orange, red, purple, blue, and then black.

Passengers were forming alliances. Certain men always sat together to play cards. Women usually gathered in one corner—near the area that formed their cabin when the curtain was drawn—and knitted while they gossiped about their destinations, their families, the life they were leaving behind. Some of the younger men would gather at the railing with their rifles and shoot at anything that moved on the passing prairie when the bluffs were low enough to see beyond the river. When the bluffs were too high, they would toss objects into the river and shoot at them as they floated by. The Army men would watch and encourage them, but they had no ammunition of their own, so they didn't participate.

Abigail Demille kept apart from the small groups of women, or perhaps it was the other way around. Far from being bored or appearing lonely, however, she watched all the activity around her with bright, inquisitive eyes. Men would buy her drinks, and she would raise the glass in thanks but only sip a little and then set the glass down. She never drained a glass other than a glass of water. Occasionally she would stroll past the card games and take in everything in a minimum of time—who was winning, who was losing, who was enjoying the game, who was marking time. She never lingered behind any one card player.

The captain, at the urging of his partners in St. Louis, began taking his meals in the dining room and making himself accessible to the passengers. He was not a social person, but he felt it was his duty to promote steamboat travel when he could. It sometimes worked, sometimes didn't.

"Captain, have you been working in the trade a long time?"

"No."

"This boat seems so complicated. Did it take you a long time to learn how to run it?"

"No."

"I notice that the farther we travel, the farther the towns are apart. Will they get even farther apart past Omaha?"

"Yes."

The woman was disappointed that she hadn't been able to elicit more detailed responses to her questions. She turned her attention to the food on her plate.

An older man took up the challenge. "Captain," he said, "I much prefer travel on the Ohio River to this Missouri River."

The captain looked at the man but said nothing.

"There is a lot of settlement along the Ohio, farms, towns, businesses that cater to the boats."

No response.

"I recall one time before the war broke out when we were coming down toward the Mississippi. The captain said, 'Gentlemen, we'll be making a stop around the next bend. You are welcome to go ashore, and I'll blow a long blast when we're ready to cast off.' " This time the man didn't wait long for a response; he went on. "Well, sir, I'll tell you, we tied up next to the finest tavern I have ever had the pleasure of visiting. The ale was the finest, ice cold, dark, and clear, and the barmaids were the loveliest creatures to behold. Is there such a place somewhere on the Missouri?"

"No, there isn't."

"I see. Pity." And this man likewise gave up and turned his attention to his glass of beer.

Then a soft voice spoke, so quiet that some at the table might not have heard it. It was Abigail Demille, seated four chairs away from the captain.

"Captain, forgive me, but I have noticed one of the stripes on your left sleeve is coming unstitched. If you have another coat to wear, I would be happy to take that one to my room and restitch it for you."

The captain was momentarily caught off guard. Although it was an innocent offer, it somehow seemed very intimate. He glanced quickly at the lovely Miss Demille, then lifted his left arm and fingered the loose stripe. Then he looked again at Miss Demille.

"Miss Demille, I'm sure our laundress can attend to it. Thank you for the offer."

"Very well, Captain. I have noticed that your staff is very competent." Abigail stood up. "I find I have time to spare, so if your staff becomes burdened with other matters, it would give me pleasure to do some sewing." As she said this, she walked past him and touched his arm. Then she was gone.

The captain looked at the people seated around him to see what they might think of this personal exchange.

"Say, Captain, I think you've made an impression on someone," said the elderly gentleman who had spoken to the captain before.

The captain rose, saying, "Please excuse me, I must return to the pilothouse." He turned and strode to the exit, not the same one Abigail had used. The men glanced at each other and grinned.

Danny was circulating around the salon, watching the card games. Riverboats were notorious for being the playing field for gamblers who liked to take advantage of naïve travelers. Danny had become adept at spotting cheaters. There was little to arouse his suspicions tonight, however.

All the doors to the outside were blocked open to allow air to circulate through the salon. The huff of the engines at eighty times a minute could be clearly heard, as could the splashing of the stern wheel. The sounds of the machinery drowned out most of the night sounds from the shore—an owl, a fish jumping and landing flat against the water, wind in the leaves—but occasionally a night sound would penetrate into the salon.

Danny heard a coyote and decided to leave the salon for a while and stand by the railing to see what else he might hear. As he exited the salon, he heard the sounds of a scuffle coming from the walkway above. He walked quickly to the stairway. As he ascended, he heard a muffled cry.

When he gained the upper deck he was struck hard in the face and nearly fell back down the stairway. He clung to the rail as he was struck again, but, ignoring the blow, pulled himself forward.

There were lamps at every stateroom door, and in their dim light Danny was able to assess his attacker. He swung once and connected solidly; the other man went down, sprang back up, and ran toward the aft end of the hurricane deck. He had to jump over a human form that was lying on the walkway—his previous victim. Danny followed, stepping over the apparently unconscious person, and caught the man near the davits that held the yawl. They exchanged blows again, and Danny went down.

The form lying on the walkway sat up. It was one of the

black maids. She screamed a long, attention-getting scream. It was clearly heard in the salon over the sounds of the machinery.

The assailant had managed to remove Danny's revolver and club him on his head with the barrel. Danny kicked out with his legs as the man stepped forward to administer another blow, and their legs got tangled. The man went over the railing. He bounced off the railing of the walkway below, landed in the dark Missouri River, and disappeared. If he struggled in the water, the sounds of that struggle were lost.

The captain had come to the sound of the scream and was helping the maid to her feet.

"What happened, Eleanor?"

"I was comin' to make up the room, and when I done opened the door, that galoot was stealin' the Willises' stuff."

The captain looked toward the stern. He saw only Danny, who was slowly getting to his feet. The first mate had heard the scream from the bow and joined the captain and Eleanor.

"Mr. Barton?"

"No, suh. One a' them deckers. I tried to stop him, but he was too big. Mistuh Barton tried to stop 'im too."

"Where did he go?"

"I reckon he done went swimmin'."

Danny walked slowly back to the captain. His face was bloody and bruised.

"Captain," the mate asked, "do you want me to call man overboard?"

"I think not. Let's see to Eleanor and Mr. Barton."

It was at this time that the door to Abigail Demille's stateroom opened and she stepped out wearing a robe. She had been asleep. The first person she saw was Eleanor, whose right eye was swelling shut.

"Oh, my goodness, you dear! Let me see you." She cradled one hand around the maid's face and tilted it to the light.

The maid, a former slave, was embarrassed. "I be all right."

"Yes, I think so, but you come into my room and sit down where I can take a good look at you." Abigail took Eleanor's hand and led her into the stateroom. The captain followed as far as the door.

"Miss Demille?"

Abigail turned around. "Yes, Captain?"

"When you're satisfied that the woman is all right, would you look at Mr. Barton also." He pointed to Danny, who was leaning on the rail, still unsteady on his feet. He had two gashes on his head, which were bleeding down to his collar, and one of his eyes was swollen. When Abigail saw him for the first time, her eyebrows rose.

"Yes, certainly, Captain." She confronted Danny. "Mr. Barton, you stay right there while I make sure this young lady isn't seriously injured. Then she and I will take care of you, and I dare say, it'll take both of us." She gave the captain a look and then attended to Eleanor, who was sitting in her stateroom. The captain returned to the pilothouse.

"Miss Abigail, I gon' be all right. Let's us fix Mr. Barton up."

Abigail smiled at the woman. "That's a good idea . . . Eleanor? Is that your name?"

"Yes, ma'am. Eleanor Smith." And with that Eleanor took Danny by the arm and led him into Abigail's room to sit in the chair she had occupied. Abigail, rather than giving instructions, let Eleanor take the lead.

"I'll go get some water, Eleanor."

"Yes, ma'am, we'll be needin' that," Eleanor said, then directed her attention to Danny. "Can you see out of that eye?" she asked.

"Yeah. I'm all right. You ladies don't have to bother with me."

"You ain't all right, young fella. You jes' set still while I see what else might be tore up on you. Mercy!" Danny leaned back in the chair.

Abigail returned with a bucket of water and some towels.

The two ladies worked together to clean the dried blood from Danny's face. Eleanor was silent, but Abigail talked as they worked.

"Have you known Captain Culpepper long?" she asked.

"I served under him in the last year of the war," Danny answered. He tried not to wince as Eleanor wiped dried blood from around his eye.

"Don't be jerkin' away, Mr. Barton," Eleanor admonished. "I'm tryin' to clean your face."

Abigail took a blood-soaked towel from Eleanor and handed her one that she had rinsed and wrung out. As Eleanor worked her way around to the side of Danny's head, Abigail leaned in for a closer look.

"He still bleedin'," Eleanor said.

"Mr. Barton, I believe you're going to need stitches in your head."

"Not much chance of that until we get to Omaha," Danny said.

"Oh, I think Eleanor and I can take care of it, can't we, Eleanor?"

"If you say so, ma'am."

Abigail went to her closet and removed her black leather grip. It looked somewhat like a train case, which would have been normal onboard a steamboat, but when she opened it, it looked more like a doctor's medical bag. "Eleanor," she said, "try to get all the hair and dirt out of that wound, and I'll sew it up."

"Yes, ma'am," Eleanor said.

"Does the captain have a family?" Abigail asked Danny.

"He never talks about one. I really don't know," he answered.

Eleanor did as Abigail asked, and Abigail began stitching the laceration closed with quick, neat stitches. Danny tried without success not to wince, but Abigail didn't seem to notice.

"I suppose it would be difficult to have a family if one spent all one's time on the river," Abigail speculated. She tied off the last stitch. "There!" She and Eleanor stood back to admire their work.

"You're probably not going to want to wear your hat for a few days," Abigail said as Eleanor wrapped a bandage around Danny's head.

"I think I lost my hat," Danny said. "I lost my Colt too." He squeezed his empty holster.

It was a short walk from the pilothouse to Abigail's room. The captain returned and stood in the doorway.

"Mr. Barton, how do you feel?"

Abigail stepped back from Danny and stood next to the captain.

"I've been bounced a little, but I'm not broken." He tried to grin, but gave it up when he felt pain around his swollen eye. Abigail watched the captain's face when Danny answered, but his expression rarely changed and it didn't this time as well.

"I suggest you spend the rest of the night in your room. I'll have Weedeater take over for you." He made a mental note to warn Danny that he did not expect him to be overpowered by one man, and that Danny should make the necessary adjustments in his habits and equipment to make sure it didn't happen again.

"I'll get my other Colt and will be available to help Weedeater if he has trouble," Danny said.

The captain examined Danny's battered head. "Very well, Mr. Barton, sleep well." He turned his attention to Abigail Demille. "Miss Demille, you have talents that we have been unaware of. Those are professional-looking stitches."

"Why, thank you, Captain," Abigail said in her soft, clear voice. "It's a skill I learned many years ago."

"Mr. Barton and I are grateful to you," the captain said.

Abigail smiled at the captain and then at Danny. Then, as if something suddenly occurred to her, she turned back to the captain as Danny made his departure.

"Captain Culpepper, could I persuade you to have supper with me tomorrow night? Away from the other passengers?" She hastened to add, "I mean, at a small table in the dining room?"

"That is often a busy time for me, Miss DeMille."

"But you do eat, do you not?" she asked with a twinkle in her eye.

"Yes."

"Tomorrow evening then?"

"It would be my pleasure, Miss Demille," the captain answered without smiling and bowed slightly as he left to return to the pilothouse.

Chapter Seven

Jack Galloway closed his ledger with a satisfied smirk. His accounts all balanced, in spite of the fact that several hundred dollars had found its way into his pockets. A fringe benefit of the scheme for which he had been hired, a scheme for which he had been given false references.

Galloway closed and locked the window through which he conducted business, and then he slipped out of his office and locked the door behind him. He wanted to stroll through the *Clinton* and begin surveying the steamer for weaknesses, flaws, areas of vulnerability.

His first efforts were to locate the steering cables where they passed through the main salon from the pilothouse above to the cargo bay below. He was disappointed to discover that they were cable rather than rope. He had been told that most steamers used rope-steering cables, and that certainly had been true only a few years before, but no longer. Even a heavy ax would not cut through the cables unless repeated blows were employed. He went to the cargo bay.

The *Clinton* had two boilers over one firebox on each side of the forward cargo bay. He watched the firemen stoking the fireboxes with cordwood. The cordwood was stacked near enough to the boilers to allow it to be fed into the fireboxes without undue effort, but not near enough to be at risk of receiving a spark. The area in front of the firebox doors was brick. There were fire buckets in several locations. An

accidental fire in the area of the boilers on the *Clinton* was
unlikely.

Galloway walked down the center of the cargo bay, glancing
at the cargo stacked on both sides. Whiskey and gunpowder
was stored below. A fire in the hold would be disastrous, but it
was highly unlikely. The entire hold was damp, and sparks
would not likely gain a foothold there.

At the aft end of the cargo bay was the engine room, which
spanned the vessel from one side to the other. There were two
engines, one on each side, each driving a long hardwood strut
called a pitman arm, which penetrated the wall at the stern and
was attached to the stern wheel. Galloway didn't know it, but a
good engineer could keep the boat moving with just one engine.

B-watch was on duty, it being six in the evening. Peter Van
Dusen was the B-watch engineer, and he didn't particularly care
for visitors. The purser was an officer equal in rank to an engineer, so he didn't order Galloway to leave.

"What business do you have here?" Van Dusen asked
brusquely.

Galloway had a story ready. "I've never seen the engine
room on the *Clinton* or on any sternwheeler," he said.

At that moment the engine room telegraph rang for full
speed. Each engine on the *Clinton* was equipped with both a
variable cutoff valve and a fixed cutoff valve. The fixed cutoff
gave maximum power but was wasteful of steam. Normal travel
was with the variable cutoff valve. Van Dusen changed the
starboard engine over to the fixed cutoff valve while his striker
did the same with the larboard engine. He wore heavy leather
gloves to insulate his hands from the hot valve gear. In just
a minute, the pilothouse rang for reduced power, and Van
Dusen and his striker reversed their actions. Van Dusen syn-
chronized the two engines and then took off his heavy gloves
to cool his hands.

"That's engine room work, Galloway. Do you want anything

else?" Van Dusen was clearly unhappy at having to make corrections so rapidly.

"I guess not." Galloway wanted to know more about the operation of the engines but didn't want to ask, and it was obvious Van Dusen didn't want him hanging around. He made a note to himself to come back when A-watch was on duty. Perhaps the other engineer would be more cooperative. He walked out of the engine room and made his way upstairs to his office.

The sun was setting and the kitchen staff was making preparations for the evening meal. The long table was set with tablecloths, plates, glasses, silverware, candles, and napkins. Some of the smaller tables in the bar area were likewise set, and one of these had a reserved sign on it. The stateroom passengers could eat at the table or ask for food to be sent to their cabins. As soon as they were served, the passengers who had berths in the main salon could sit down. After these people had eaten, the roustabouts, maids, and kitchen staff could eat, and persons with deck passage could also come up to the dining room.

There were four meals a day on the *Clinton*: breakfast at sunrise, lunch at eleven o'clock, dinner at three o'clock, and supper after sunset. Officers, stateroom passengers, cabin passengers, roustabouts, maids, kitchen staff, and enlisted men were all furnished with meals. Deckers had to buy their own or cook on the bow. Culpepper was committed to seeing that everyone onboard was fed adequately, and this set the *Clinton* apart from many other steamboats on the Missouri.

Galloway instructed a kitchen worker to bring him a plate and then let himself into his office. He needed to make contact with his assistant without arousing suspicions and wasn't sure how best to proceed. It would be several weeks before they got beyond Omaha, so there was no reason to get anxious. But he was. The *Clinton* was a well-run, well-maintained vessel, and scuttling it might be more of a challenge than he had anticipated. He needed to talk strategy with his fellow conspirator.

Galloway took a piece of paper and wrote *I need to see you to discuss business.* He didn't like this and tore the paper in half and threw it away. He thought for a moment and then wrote *Come to my office after the ladies' cabin is set up.* This seemed to satisfy him. He folded the paper twice and put it into his pocket. Then he went to the window and looked out over the room to see if the intended recipient was present.

The table with the reserved sign on it now had one diner, Abigail Demille. She sat alone, observing the rest of the room. Passengers were finding seats at the main table: Army officers, off-duty vessel officers, first- and second-class passengers. Galloway watched with interest from his office to see who might join Miss Demille. She was the jewel among the passengers and always attracted attention, yet she seemed to not be aware of their interest. A few minutes later, Captain Culpepper entered the room. Instead of taking his customary seat at the head of the main table, he walked stiffly to the table where Abigail Demille sat, spoke a few words, and sat down opposite her. Galloway smirked to himself, patted the folded note in his pocket, and began eating the meal that had been brought to him.

"I'm sorry I'm late, Miss Demille," the captain said. "Please forgive me. There were matters that required my attention."

"Not at all, Captain. I feel very honored to have you sit with me when so many other passengers also value your company." She smiled warmly; the captain said nothing.

An alert waiter had seen the captain enter the room and hurried to the table to see to his dinner order. After taking his and Miss Demille's order, the waiter left for the kitchen.

Abigail was not about to let the captain sit uncomfortably in silence. "How far have we come from St. Louis, Captain?"

"About two hundred and fifty miles," he answered.

"Could we have come this far this fast in a stagecoach?"

"Yes, farther, actually."

"Travel by stagecoach seems to me to be much more uncomfortable and dangerous though," Abigail supposed.

"Yes, I think that is so."

Abigail hoped he would elaborate, but he didn't. She continued.

"A railroad train would also be faster, wouldn't it?"

"Yes."

"And not nearly as risky as a stagecoach?"

"That is so."

"I once rode a stagecoach from Baltimore to Philadelphia."

The captain said nothing for a few minutes, then, just as Abigail had decided she would try another subject in hopes of leading him into a more social conversation, he spoke.

"I have ridden a horse on that road. Was it a long trip by stagecoach?"

"Yes, two days, and we had to take a ferry across the Susquehanna River in a horrible wind and rainstorm. I was only a little girl."

"Before the war, then," the captain concluded.

Abigail smiled. "Yes, long before the war."

The captain might have graciously said that she looked too young to have been alive long before the war, but he didn't know how to say such things and make them sound natural and appropriate. He stayed silent.

"What did you do before the war, Captain?"

"I joined the Army in 1843."

"And you served through the war?"

"Yes. Although I did not attend West Point, I attained the rank of colonel."

"So you were in command of a regiment? A thousand men?"

The captain was impressed. Miss Demille had knowledge of military organization. "No," he answered. "I was a lieutenant colonel, second in command, until our colonel was killed in 1864 and never replaced. And our regiment was never at full strength."

"Still, it was quite an accomplishment to attain that rank. I have heard that it was difficult to retain rank after the war ended." Abigail put her hand to her throat. "I'm sorry, Captain. That remark was somewhat inappropriate."

"Not at all, Miss Demille. I resigned my commission in order to buy this boat."

"It must be quite different for you after twenty-two years in the Army."

"It's a much smaller command."

"And, one would hope, fewer life-and-death decisions for you."

"Yes, certainly."

Abigail was thoughtful for a moment as she considered that reply and what she wanted to say next.

"But, after all those years in the Army, you're still away from home most of the time. That hasn't changed, has it?"

"This is my home," the captain said and glanced around to reinforce his words.

Abigail also looked around briefly. "Do you have no family, Captain?"

"No."

Abigail wanted to know more. "It seems peculiar that a man of your ability would not have found a wife."

The captain stiffened and then replied, "I was married early in my career but I was . . . preoccupied, ambitious. She left me many years ago."

Abigail feared she might have gone too far, but before she could think of what to say next, their supper arrived.

Chapter Eight

It was 11:45 P.M., and Robert Pruitt had just come to the pilothouse to take over the watch. The mates were conferring in the cargo bay, and the engineers were changing the watch in their area, the engine room. Danny Barton was the only person in the pilothouse other than the two pilots. He enjoyed listening to the technical details of piloting that were invariably discussed when Felden and Pruitt changed watch.

"Mr. Pruitt, you'll have to deal with the Sorensen Rapids this watch. They're fifteen minutes ahead." Charles Felden put one finger on the chart that was always spread out on a table next to the wheel.

Pruitt rubbed the sleep from his eyes. Sleeping in three-and-a-half-hour sessions was not a natural thing for the human body, and it was taking its toll. "The channel goes along the right bank most of the way through, as I remember," he said.

"Not exactly. I marked the channel deviations that we found last month coming down. You might want to check your notes against the chart."

"All right."

"The rudders were sluggish for a short period. It cleared up when I had them hard over a few minutes later," Felden said. "After that I tested them several times where the river was wide, and they responded normally."

"Perhaps some driftwood jammed between the rudders and the stern," Pruitt speculated.

"Probably," Felden answered. "Brown removed several covers on the cableway and found nothing wrong."

"Which direction did you have the wheel hard over when it cleared?" Pruitt asked.

"Starboard."

The second hand came up to the twelve on the pilothouse clock. Felden rang eight bells and stepped back from the wheel, and Pruitt stepped up. He watched the river for a moment and turned the wheel one direction and then the other. He was satisfied with the response and nodded to Felden as the senior pilot left the pilothouse to get some sleep.

Pruitt held the wheel with one hand while he leaned over the chart and then looked at Felden's log.

"What the heck!" he exclaimed. "We can't be there if we're fifteen miles from Sorensen Rapids."

Pruitt allowed himself a quick glance in the direction Felden had just taken, but Felden was out of sight. Barton held his breath, not sure of what Pruitt was going to have to do to solve his problem, but fairly certain there was nothing he could do to help.

Pruitt looked at the chart again and then out both windows at the darkness. The river's surface was visible to about two hundred feet ahead, but only dimly. Pruitt checked the log again. He was lost.

Suddenly the *Clinton* lurched to the left, nearly knocking Barton and Pruitt to the floor. Pruitt looked out of the right side of the pilothouse. In the glow of the side lanterns, he could see a massive boulder. The prow of the *Clinton* had glanced off this boulder. It was fortunate that it had not hit straight on, but the troubles were not over. While Pruitt had been distracted, the *Clinton* had entered the Sorensen Rapids at the swiftest part and, after hitting the boulder, was yawing to the left in the powerful current.

The silhouettes of the trees and the taller bushes along the banks gave Pruitt the visual clues that the boat was in the wrong attitude. He spun the wheel to the right. He needed more drive to push against the rudders to correct the yaw and make gains against the current, but the engines were already at the maximum available while on the variable cutoff. He rang for full speed. With the boat's attitude not lined up with the current, he was in danger of driving the boat out of the channel.

The captain had awakened when the *Clinton* struck the boulder and now entered the pilothouse. It had taken him only seconds to pull on his pants and boots and button his coat. He said nothing while taking up his usual position against the back wall of the pilothouse. The second mate, David Erickson, also entered the pilothouse.

"There's a leadsman on the bow, Mr. Pruitt," he said quickly. "He's getting eleven feet, but there are some rocks."

Pruitt cursed. The *Clinton* was not turning back into the current fast enough. He rang the engine room for half reverse and made ready to spin the wheel to the opposite lock as soon as he heard the engines would stop.

It would have been an incredible breach of faith and a violation of the rules of the steamboat trade for the captain to have interfered at any time with the navigation of the vessel. Pruitt was a certified pilot, and the safe navigation of the *Clinton* was his responsibility until the change of watch, when it would fall on Felden. The captain said nothing. Except for the vein standing out on his forehead, one might have thought he was indifferent to Pruitt's predicament. Nor could Erickson, the mate, do anything; even a suggestion would have been out of place, but his face was not as emotionless as the captain's. He opened one of the pilothouse windows to receive the call from the leadsman, which he relayed to Pruitt.

"Still eleven feet, Mr. Pruitt." There was a hint of a question in his voice that he hoped would cue Pruitt.

The engines stopped, and Pruitt spun the wheel to the left

as the paddlewheel began turning in reverse. Now the *Clinton* was no longer fighting the current, but was drifting down.

If you throw a stick into a stream, it will invariably turn until it is crosscurrent and remain that way as it journeys downstream. This was the position of the *Clinton* as its forward progress through the water slowed. Response to the rudders became even more sluggish.

"Ten feet, Mr. Pruitt!"

Pruitt looked toward the left shore and to the right. Although he could see the outlines of the treetops, he could not tell where he was in the river. "Mr. Erickson, get an anchor crew on the bow with the big anchor and standby!" This was what Erickson was waiting for, and he left the pilothouse shouting the order. Too late.

The *Clinton* drifted backward over a submerged rock, and the paddles made a *tat-tat-tat-tat-tat* sound. The rock somehow missed the rudders, but then the stern of the *Clinton* momentarily dragged on the rock, turning the steamer even more crosscurrent. Pruitt rang the engine room to stop the engines. His only hope to avoid total disaster was the anchor crew, and he could only watch helplessly from the pilothouse as they rigged the anchor and threw it over.

The anchor found the bottom and wedged in tight. The *Clinton* turned into the current and stopped. Pruitt leaned out the window and shouted to Erickson on the bow. "Start the doctor engine and pull the hatches! Stand by to pump the hold!"

Erickson was ahead of Pruitt. As soon as the anchor had been thrown over, Erickson had rounded up more roustabouts, and they had removed several hatches even before Pruitt had given the command. There was freight on top of some of the hatches and this had to be moved; Erickson had a big crew working now. Looking through the first hatch opening, Erickson saw what he had hoped he wouldn't see. There was water in the hold.

The pump, driven by the doctor engine, was hard-piped to several low spots in the hold. Once it was started, the engineer opened valves at Erickson's direction. There was a solid output of muddy water from the pump. Erickson used a long, marked stick to measure the water depth in the hold and then sent a roustabout to the pilothouse with that information. Next, he hurried to the bow to assess the effectiveness of the anchor.

The anchor line was snubbed to a bit on the bow. Erickson leaned over the bow and wrapped his hand around the anchor line. By so doing, he could feel if the anchor was moving across the river bottom, and he decided it was not. He instructed the roustabouts to drop a small anchor straight down off the bow, and when it hit bottom, feed out ten more feet of line. This was a tattletale—if the *Clinton* dragged the big anchor, the line on the small anchor would go taut.

Erickson returned to the cargo bay and the hatch where he had measured the water's depth. He measured again and found that the pump had gained on the leak; there was an inch less water in the hold. He sent two roustabouts into the hold to find the damage and went to the pilothouse to tell Pruitt.

The engineer had clearly heard the paddlewheel strike the submerged rock. He set the brake on the wheel and found some roustabouts to help him perform an inspection of the paddles. As luck would have it, the damaged buckets, ten in all, had been stopped near the top, and Van Dusen, after pinning the wheel to make doubly sure it wouldn't turn, climbed up over the side of the paddlewheel with a lantern to see how extensive the damage was.

By the light of the lantern, Van Dusen found the damage the rock had caused. The ten damaged buckets all had splintered edges, and three had significant amounts of wood missing. He climbed back to the walkway and returned to the engine room, where he told his striker that he was going to the pilothouse to report. He arrived there just as Erickson was giving his report.

"We're looking for the damage, Mr. Pruitt. There is at least one leak, but the pump is able to get ahead of the leak."

"All right, David, thanks," Pruitt replied. He was an unhappy man and still hadn't reasoned out what went wrong. Erickson left to supervise the pumping. "What do you have, Mr. Van Dusen?" Pruitt asked the engineer.

"Three buckets with significant damage, Mr. Pruitt. The wheel is already pinned. If we're going to be here more than an hour, we can complete repairs in the dark without difficulty." Buckets were easily replaced, and all steamboats carried spares.

"All right, Peter, start the repairs. We'll need maximum efficiency to get started against this current." Van Dusen left to organize a repair crew.

Now there were only the captain, the pilot, and Danny Barton in the pilothouse. After an uncomfortably long silence, the captain spoke.

"What happened, Mr. Pruitt?"

Pruitt knew what had happened; he just didn't know why. He began to recount the events.

"We struck a boulder and were thrown off course. Before I could straighten her out, we struck a submerged rock, must have hung up momentarily, and the current put us farther out of attitude." He took a quick look at the captain. "The big anchor is holding while we assess the damage and make repairs."

"Was the rock charted?"

"Not if we're at the position reported at change of watch." Pruitt went to the chart and put his finger on a section of river.

"What position is indicated in the log?"

Pruitt looked at the log. Felden's last entry had been at 11:47 P.M. and listed the *Clinton* as one-half mile below the Sorensen Rapids. But Pruitt clearly remembered Felden saying the Sorensen Rapids were fifteen miles ahead. Fifteen miles! That didn't make sense. The *Clinton* should not have entered the rapids until well into his watch. Pruitt realized he had not given the change of watch and exchange of information the attention that was required. But he had to defend himself with what he believed were the facts.

"The log shows that the *Clinton* was nearing the rapids at the change of watch, but Felden told me were fifteen miles below them." His eyes didn't meet the captain's.

The captain's voice was flat, scarcely betraying his anger, and in control. "See to the repairs, Mr. Pruitt, and get under way." He strode out of the pilothouse with not a glance to Barton.

When Barton was sure that the captain was in his cabin, he leaned toward Pruitt and spoke in a low voice. "Robert, Charles Felden said we would enter the Sorensen Rapids in fifteen minutes, not fifteen miles."

Although this was what Pruitt had been fearful of, he still wanted to believe that Felden had misinformed him. "And you intend to tell the captain this?"

The security officer looked into Pruitt's eyes, feeling some disappointment. It seemed to him that Pruitt was not ready to accept responsibility for the incident. "Only if I'm asked," he said.

Chapter Nine

The *Barnard Clinton* arrived in Kansas City on a late Saturday afternoon. Pruitt eased the *Clinton* into place at the wharf without difficulty. Captain Culpepper had been waiting for the opportunity to talk to his pilots without the distraction of having one of them having to navigate.

"Mr. Pruitt, when Mr. Felden comes on watch at eight, both of you report to my cabin."

"Yes, sir," Pruitt said.

"Have the first mate stand by in the pilothouse."

"Yes, sir."

The captain left the pilothouse and walked around to stand in front, looking down on the bow. There was some freight to be offloaded, and the roustabouts were bringing that out of the cargo bay as a teamster backed his wagon down the starboard stage.

There were also some passengers waiting to board. The purser set up his table on the bow and beckoned them down the larboard stage. There was a family waiting patiently at the shore end of the stage, but they were shouldered aside by five rough-looking men. The captain frowned as he watched the men stride arrogantly down the stage to the purser. Each of the men was carrying a grip, and each of them had a pistol stuck in his belt. Two of them were carrying carbines.

If the five had been former cavalry men, they would have had holsters for their pistols. If they were buffalo hunters, they would have had long rifles instead of carbines. If they were trail herders, they would have had saddles. The captain couldn't guess what their purpose in traveling up the river might be, but he thought they might bring trouble.

Danny thought so too. He was on the bow for the express purpose of watching the passengers coming onboard. He stepped between the five men and the purser.

His face was still swollen and discolored from the fight, and he wasn't wearing a hat. He was taller than any of the five men. His appearance caused them to stop when he held his hand up in front of them, and there began a loud discourse, which the captain couldn't quite make out. The two men closest to Danny dropped their grips on the stage and put their hands on their belt pistols as the conversation continued. The men pressed closer to Danny and began to flank him.

Danny was wearing his pistol in its holster, but he had made no move to put it in hand. His posture, however, betrayed no inclination to back down as he leaned forward into the group to explain something to them that they obviously did not appreciate. The five men suddenly backed up a step and fell silent. The captain observed that now Weedeater was standing beside Danny with a shotgun, his hand on the grip and his finger near the trigger. Danny pointed up the stage to the man with the family and beckoned him down, but the man would have none of it. He shook his head slowly and put his arms around two of his children while his wife picked up the smallest one. They held their ground, not wanting to be the cause of a disagreement between seven armed men. Danny shrugged and stepped aside to let the five men make arrangements for passage with the purser.

As the five walked down the stage, Weedeater leaned over to Danny and said, "Danny, don't let people like that surround you. I'd have had to shoot you to shoot them."

Danny nodded as he watched the men book passage with

the purser. It was good advice, and he felt sure that he wasn't
through with the five men.

At 7:45 the captain was in the pilothouse when Felden and the
rest of the A-watch came on duty.

"Mr. Erickson, take the pilothouse until eight bells, then
turn it over to Mr. Allenby. The pilots and I are going to have
a meeting."

"Yes, sir," Erickson said.

The men gathered in the pilothouse exchanged glances as
the captain led the two pilots out and to his cabin. As the cabin
door was closed, the captain began.

"Mr. Pruitt, you have put the *Clinton* on the bottom
again."

Technically, the *Clinton* hadn't run aground, but Pruitt did
not challenge the captain's interpretation. "Yes, sir."

"We lost two hours, three paddles, and very nearly the vessel." The captain didn't need to add that in the dark and in the
rapids, there would probably have been loss of life also. Pruitt
said nothing. He tried to meet the captain's penetrating gaze
but faltered and looked away. Felden said nothing. The captain continued.

"What I find interesting is that this incident occurred so soon
after the change of watch." Now the captain looked at Felden,
who didn't waver. "I can only assume that the exchange of information was flawed. Is that correct?"

Felden nodded.

"Yes, sir," Pruitt answered.

"Very well. You may go, Mr. Pruitt. I'll be talking to you
later. I now want to talk to Mr. Felden alone."

Pruitt left the captain's cabin to find his own and get some
sleep. Felden stayed behind, wondering if the captain was going to place some of the blame on him. It would have been
unjust, but he was prepared to accept it. He knew what kind

of pilot he was, and unfortunately, he also knew what kind of pilot Robert Pruitt was.

"Mr. Felden, I'm going to tell you something that I want you to keep absolutely to yourself." Felden nodded his acceptance of the condition.

The captain didn't waste time getting to the point.

"Robert Pruitt is my son."

This was astounding news, but Felden remained silent.

"I was aware that he had become a pilot, and when Singletary left, I sent for him as a replacement." The captain leaned over to look out the small window in his cabin, then straightened and continued. "My wife left me when he was only five years old, taking him to live with her parents. I have had little to do with his upbringing and, in fact, have not seen him since some months before the war."

Both men were still standing as they had been since entering the cabin. There were two chairs in the room, and it seemed to Felden that they should sit down to continue the discussion, one-sided though it may be. He spoke for the first time.

"Let's sit down, Captain," he said, and indicated the chairs.

"No. Another time I think I'd like that, but I have only one more thing to say."

"Yes, sir?"

"Robert has demonstrated his lack of competence twice. If you had done the same, I would allow you only one more mistake. Give him the benefit of your experience, even to the point of becoming overbearing. I would like him to be successful, but I won't put lives and my vessel at risk. If he fails again, I will put him ashore, and he will be made to understand that."

"Yes, sir." Felden tried to read the captain's face, but he could not tell if the captain was sad, mad, or simply taking care of business.

"You may go, Charles," the captain said. It was the first time Felden had heard the captain use his first name. He nodded and left the cabin to take over the watch. The captain sat at his desk and made some notes in a book. Then, realizing that it had become quite dark, he descended to the main salon.

Abigail Demille was sitting at the long table when the captain walked in. She had not been able to have a conversation with the captain since their supper together two nights previous. The captain took his customary seat at the head of the table and then noticed Abigail, two chairs down from him. It was late, most of the passengers had eaten, so the chairs separating them were empty. Abigail was not quite finished with her meal, and she briefly considered carrying her plate and silverware to the place next to the captain.

As if reading her thoughts, the captain asked, "May I join you, Miss Demille?"

Before she could answer, the second mate, Erickson, came up to the captain's side. The captain glanced at Abigail to try to discern if she had been about to answer positively, and then he devoted his attention to the mate.

"Captain, we have unloaded the freight that was consigned to Kansas City."

"Very well. Is there freight to be loaded?"

"Yes, sir. There is more Army freight. At least forty tons."

"That's good. Tell the pilot so he can keep the nose off the bottom while it's being loaded."

"Yes, sir. There are also five Army personnel coming onboard."

"Rank?"

"Four enlisted men and a major."

"The cabins are all booked. Isn't that so?"

"Yes, sir."

"Tell the major to put his gear in my cabin. We can't have an Army officer sleeping in the main salon."

"Yes, sir."

"Thank you, Mr. Erickson. Carry on."

The second mate left the main salon to carry out the captain's orders.

The captain again turned his attention to Abigail Demille. She gestured at the chair next to hers.

"Captain?" she invited.

The captain nodded and seated himself next to her. Then he beckoned to a waiter.

"The business of the riverboat goes on at all hours, doesn't it?" she asked.

"Yes, it certainly does."

"Does it become tiresome?"

"Not at all. I prefer activity. I enjoy making decisions."

Abigail was silent while she considered this statement. Then she had another question. "I would suppose that the decisions you make in operating a steamboat are less critical than the ones you made during the war. Is that so?"

"Yes, beyond doubt."

"What could happen that would require you to make the same kinds of decisions that you made during the war?"

This was a question that would have made most men raise their eyebrows, but the captain answered without changing his expression. "The *Barnard Clinton* is a hotel and a warehouse in the wilderness. The risks would seem to be great, but both the vessel and the crew are exceptionally capable. You are as safe aboard the *Clinton* as you would be in a hotel in St. Louis."

"Oh, I didn't mean to give the impression that I was anxious about my safety aboard the *Barnard Clinton*. I was merely curious to know if there were any . . . What worried you the most?"

"No offense taken, Miss Demille," he said. "If there's one thing that keeps me from becoming overly relaxed, I suppose . . ." The captain paused as he observed the five rough passengers enter the main salon and seat themselves. He didn't finish the sentence. "Would you excuse me, Miss DeMille. More business, I'm afraid."

Captain Culpepper walked through the main salon to the purser's office.

"Mr. Galloway, let me see your passenger manifest."

Galloway laid a ledger on the counter separating him from the captain and opened it to the most recent page of entries. The captain looked at the list of names and put his finger on one group.

"Are these the names of those five men?" he asked.

Galloway twisted his head around to help him read upside down. "Yes, I believe so," he said.

The captain read the names under his breath. "Gary Whitmore, John Whitmore, Harold Whitmore, Donald McGill, Peter McGill." He turned to assess the two groups of brothers seated at the table and saw nothing but trouble. He started to return the ledger to Galloway, and then he looked at the booking arrangements for each of the men.

"These men are registered as deck passengers. Were they not told they were to eat at third call? And pay for their meals?"

"I must have made a mistake, Captain. I'm sure they registered as regular passengers."

The captain looked at Galloway long and hard. "Bring your accounts and your cash to my cabin before you retire, Mr. Galloway."

Galloway tried to look offended. "Captain, I don't . . ."

"See to it, Mr. Galloway." The captain turned sharply and walked back to his seat. Abigail Demille had left the dining room and apparently returned to her cabin. The captain resignedly sat down at the head of the table and again beckoned a waiter.

A U.S. Army major approached the captain, and Culpepper motioned for him to be seated. In no time the two were engaged in conversation about the Army, the recent war, the Indian campaigns, and many other military matters. The captain reflected that this conversation was at least as interesting as one would have been with the beautiful Miss Demille, if not as pleasant.

Chapter Ten

At eleven thirty P.M., Captain Culpepper, who had been working at his desk under a low lamp, left his cabin and the sleeping Army major and entered the pilothouse.

Charles Felden was redrawing one of his river charts, adding this year's notes. Danny Barton was leaning over the chart table, observing. Steve Allenby, the first mate, entered just after the captain. Felden made a final mark on his chart and then rolled it up.

"Is the freight all onboard, Mr. Allenby?" asked the captain.

"No, sir. We've had to shift some of the other freight to keep her on her marks. When it's all onboard, she'll be about six inches low fore and aft."

"Is all this freight consigned to Fort Benton?"

"Most of it."

Although the extra freight meant more revenue for the *Clinton*, it also meant that navigation of the upper Missouri would be even more difficult.

"Well," the captain mused, "we'll be offloading the rails and spikes at Omaha. That will bring her up."

"Yes, sir."

Pruitt and his mate entered the pilothouse.

The captain addressed Barton. "Mr. Barton, you had a confrontation with five men on the stage this afternoon."

"Yes, Captain," Barton acknowledged. "They pushed an

immigrant family to one side. I wanted them to know they needed better manners onboard the *Clinton*."

"And then you let them board." It wasn't a question; it was a statement.

"You can't make money if I turn passengers away." The security officer was not apologetic.

"No," the captain agreed. "They'll bear watching, however."

"I intend to, Captain."

"Very well. Gentlemen, we'll cast off tomorrow afternoon at one. The midmorning watch will split at ten, so that everyone will have the opportunity to attend church in Kansas City. The watches will be inverted after that time. B-watch will come on duty at noon."

The men exchanged glances, but no one was entirely surprised. The captain always encouraged church attendance. The captain continued.

"As soon as the freight is stowed and the *Clinton* is ready to cast off, all of you may retire for the night. I wouldn't want any of my crew to fall asleep during church services." It was the nearest thing to humor that any of the men had ever heard from the captain, but they all kept straight faces, as did the captain. "Mr. Barton and the roustabout Weedeater will take turns in the pilothouse during that time."

Steve Allenby was the first to speak. "Mr. Erickson, I'll stay on to help with the freight. Then we'll all get to bed earlier."

"Thanks, Steve," Erickson said. "Let's get to it then." The two men left the pilothouse to attend to the last of the loading.

Felden spoke next. "Mr. Pruitt, the wind is holding her off the bank, so there is no problem with settling into the bank during loading. It bears watching. We've lengthened the shorelines once."

"Very well, Mr. Felden. You might as well retire now. If things go well, I'll not be far behind you," Pruitt said. Felden nodded and left the pilothouse, leaving only the captain, Danny Barton, and Robert Pruitt.

"Mr. Barton," the captain said, "find Weedeater and explain to him what is expected. I desire to speak to Mr. Pruitt alone."

"Yes, sir," Barton said and left the pilothouse.

The captain wasted no time getting to the point with his junior pilot.

"Mr. Pruitt, through inattention or bad choices, or both, you have twice put this vessel at risk."

Pruitt said nothing. He might have made a defense for his mistakes, but he knew the captain would never allow him the time to explain what he thought was more complex than the simple error it appeared to be. The captain could have pointed out that the voyage had more than enough inherent risk without adding the incompetence of a pilot, but he had enough respect for Pruitt's intelligence to eschew this. The disciplinary discussion was therefore brief.

"If another incident occurs, I'll put you ashore."

Pruitt remained silent. Barton and Weedeater appeared at the door to the pilothouse. The captain waved them away. Pruitt wondered what was coming next. The captain folded his arms across his chest, looked down at the floor for a moment, then spoke.

"We've had no chance to speak privately. I was sorry to hear of your mother's death."

"I doubted that you were aware," Pruitt said.

"I regularly correspond with Reverend Richardson, the pastor who performed our wedding ceremony," the captain said by way of explanation.

Pruitt stared at the floor. "Her marriage to Mr. Pruitt was a good one. He's a good man."

"She was a good woman."

"Yes."

"Robert, I couldn't have been more pleased when I heard you had gained certification. I think you have the makings of a first-class pilot."

"Thank you. I guess."

"I'm ready to give you any help you need, but I can't accept performance that risks lives."

"I wouldn't expect you to."

"Just do your job. You'll be fine."

"Yes, sir."

While this conversation was going on, another dialogue was taking place in a corner of the cargo bay.

"This blasted boat is going to be difficult," Jack Galloway whispered.

"What do you mean?" his accomplice asked.

"It's well built and well run. Most of these barges are just accidents waiting to happen. This one is different."

"Why not just blow it up?" the accomplice asked.

"They want it to look natural."

"Riverboats blow up all the time."

"Do you want to get paid?" Galloway was exasperated. "We won't get the rest of our money if we don't do what they want."

"We have at least a week before we get past Omaha. I'll see what I can find out about boiler explosions."

Galloway was mollified. "All right. A boiler explosion that put a hole in the hull would be perfect."

"Here's another possibility. Did you see the five men who boarded at K.C.?"

"Of course I did. I booked them." Galloway didn't bother telling his accomplice that he had skimmed their fare and nearly gotten fired because of it.

"They're stupid but mean and tough. It would be easy to use them to create a problem for the boat."

Galloway raised his eyebrows. "You already have them sized?"

"Yeah. No mystery there. They could be useful tools."

"So you can pull their trigger if we want?"

"Easily."

"But will you know what they'll do?" Galloway was more than a little skeptical.

"You don't have to know which way a wild horse will turn when you put a greenhorn on him. You just know the greenhorn's going to eat some dirt."

"All right." Galloway was still not convinced, but he filed all the information away. "Let's get out of here."

Chapter Eleven

Robert Pruitt attended the same Kansas City church as his father, but the two men sat apart. The service had started at ten A.M., so he was a few minutes late, being on an abbreviated watch until that time. At the conclusion of the service he walked back to the waterfront and boarded the *Barnard Clinton*. He went to the cabin that he shared with Charles Felden and sat alone for a while before straightening his tie, donning his cap, and reporting to the pilothouse.

The Missouri River at Kansas City was in the form of a bight. The river came from the north, accepted the waters of the Kansas River from the west, and then bent around over about a mile to flow back toward the northeast. The current had widened the river at the bottom of this bight, carving a deep channel near the southern shore, leaving the northern shore inaccessible to large vessels because of the extensive shallows. The *Clinton* was berthed along this southernmost portion of the river, heading southwest. So also were the *Kansas City Star* and the *Pawnee Chief*, to the west and east respectively, bracketing the *Clinton* close in. The freshening midday breeze had stretched the shorelines of all three vessels like guitar strings.

Felden looked up from his chart as Pruitt entered the pilothouse.

"Did you enjoy the church services, Mr. Pruitt?"

"Yes. Very thought-provoking," he answered.

It was only half past noon, too early for the officers to gather for the change of watch, so Felden and Pruitt were alone in the pilothouse.

"The breeze is strengthening and backing, Robert. The *Pawnee Chief* put out a stern anchor, so we shouldn't expect trouble from that direction. I've put out an anchor on a short rode, but it might not hold if the wind continues to strengthen and back. The *Kansas City Star* did the same."

"Very well," Pruitt answered. He stepped out of the pilothouse to assess the situation on both sides. After a few minutes, he returned to the pilothouse.

"It seems we're in the wind shadow of the *Pawnee Chief,* and we're holding well for the moment."

"See those clouds to the west?" Felden asked.

"Yes. They shouldn't be a problem. The wind will drive them off."

Felden didn't say anything. Pruitt looked out at the clouds and then again at the steamers berthed on either side of the *Clinton.* He knew he had said something wrong.

"Isn't that the case?" he asked at last.

"No. The wind doesn't affect the clouds in that way. Rather, the clouds will pull the wind more and more strongly, and as the wind picks up, the clouds will slowly come to us, just as if they were losing a tug of war."

"So we'll get both wind and rain?"

"We'll get the wind; the rain might hold off until this evening."

"Getting out of this berth will be a challenge," Pruitt said, stating the obvious.

"Yes, it will," Felden answered.

Pruitt was silent.

"But I imagine you'll use your wheel in reverse against left rudder while a couple of roustabouts snub your mooring line and slowly pay it out." Felden looked at Pruitt over the top of his glasses. He could practically hear the wheels grinding away in Pruitt's head. At that moment the mates walked in, followed seconds later by the captain and then Danny Barton.

"We have forty-three cords of wood, David. I decided to stock up here and at Leavenworth and Atchison. After St. Joseph, there's a long stretch of river before Omaha," stated Allenby.

"Good idea," Erickson commented. "St. Joseph by Thursday, Mr. Pruitt?"

"Yes, probably so," Pruitt replied. "Mr. Erickson, do we have a two-inch line five hundred feet long? No knots?"

"No. I can put one together with a long splice."

"Can you get it done by castoff?"

Erickson involuntarily looked at the clock on the pilothouse wall even though he knew exactly what time it was. "That's still one P.M.?" he asked.

"Yes. Can you do it?"

"I'll put two men on it right away." Erickson started to leave the pilothouse to expedite the task, but Pruitt stopped him.

"Wait," Pruitt said. "When you get it done, tie it off to the starboard bow, and lead it around the mooring post between us and the *Pawnee Chief* and back to the bow. Take two turns around the bit, and assign two big roustabouts to pay it out by my signal. Send the engineer up here. Go."

Erickson left the pilothouse briskly. The other officers were silent. They hadn't seen Pruitt act this decisively before and were waiting to see what his next actions would be. Finally, the captain spoke.

"Mr. Pruitt, do you need additional time to make preparations for castoff?"

There was only the slightest hesitation in Pruitt's reply. "No, sir."

Peter Van Dusen, Pruitt's engineer, entered the pilothouse at that moment. He had still not accepted Pruitt, and the tone of his voice betrayed that fact.

"I was told to report to you," he told Pruitt.

"Yes. At castoff I want power to come up in half-revolution increments. I'll ring slow astern each time I want another half revolution."

Van Dusen folded his arms across his chest to show his disdain for the young pilot but said nothing. Pruitt continued.

"If I ring slow ahead, take a half revolution off." Pruitt wasn't going to let Van Dusen's attitude permeate the silence in the pilothouse. "Any questions, Mr. Van Dusen?"

"No."

"Very well. That will be all."

Van Dusen wanted to further demonstrate his negative feelings, but he had been dismissed, so he had no choice but to leave the pilothouse. A minute after Van Dusen left, Erickson returned.

"We'll have five hundred forty feet of two inch with two splices in a half hour, Mr. Pruitt. I have four men working on it."

"Thank you, Mr. Erickson. Begin stoking the fireboxes, and let me know when we have one hundred fifty pounds of steam." At this moment, the minute hand and the hour hand all pointed to twelve, and Felden rang the bell eight times.

"She's all yours, Mr. Pruitt. I'm going to my cabin to catch some sleep. We'll be facing the setting sun on my next watch, and I want to be rested." It was Felden's way of telling Pruitt that he didn't want or need to be disturbed; that he had confidence that Pruitt would handle castoff without incident. Felden and Allenby both left.

The captain took all this in without comment or change of expression. He speculated to himself that Felden had set up a test for Pruitt that he expected Pruitt to pass, and he knew he wouldn't have long to wait to see how accurate his assessment was. Pruitt walked out onto the pilothouse foredeck to watch the preparations he had ordered, leaving only the captain and Barton in the pilothouse.

"Any more trouble with the five men from Kansas City, Mr. Barton?"

"No, sir. They're on a short leash. Either myself or Weedeater is keeping them in sight almost constantly."

"Good idea, Mr. Barton. Any other problems?"

"Not that I've found, Captain."

The captain shifted his weight on his feet and tugged at his beard. "I myself have found a problem about which I should have made you aware."

"Sir?"

"Our purser has been skimming the profits. He knows that I know, so I don't expect him to try it again, but he is an untrustworthy element in our officer ranks. He may be another source of trouble more insidious than the five roughnecks."

"I'll keep that in mind."

"At the first hint of trouble from that quarter, I'll put him ashore or in irons."

Barton nodded his head. "I think I'll go down to the main salon and see what's going on." He enjoyed watching castoff and berthing, but he knew the captain expected him to increase his presence among the passengers. He walked out of the pilothouse as Pruitt returned.

Pruitt looked at his chart and his notes, and then he took the field glasses and trained them on a small steamer coming up from downstream. He noted their slow progress, looked at the clock, and decided they would not arrive in time to hamper his maneuvers. A young roustabout came to the pilothouse.

"I was told to come here," the young man said.

"Yes," Pruitt confirmed. "What's your name?"

"Benji," he answered.

"Benji, the first thing I will have you do is run to the hurricane deck at my command and tell the crew at the stern to pull the anchor. Return quickly. I want you to stand in front of the pilothouse to relay my signals to the crew on the mooring line. When I ask for them to hold position, raise both fists over your head. Let me see you do it." The roustabout did as he was asked, and Pruitt was satisfied. "When I want them to let out more line, point both arms toward the mooring. Do it." The roustabout complied. "Very well," Pruitt said.

Erickson returned. "We'll have one hundred fifty pounds any minute, Mr. Pruitt."

"That's good, David. Let's show off for the town. Run all our colors up."

"All right," the mate replied before leaving the pilothouse again.

While all this was going on the wind strength had increased, and the wind was now coming from the southeast. Pruitt made those entries into his log. It was five minutes before one P.M. Pruitt made one more trip around the outside of the pilothouse to check all sides of the *Clinton* and then stepped in once more.

"All right," he told the roustabout. "Tell them to get the anchor up."

The anchor off the stern had been dropped with a trip line on a buoy. Pruitt had given the captain of the *Pawnee Chief* a bottle of whiskey to enlist the help of two of his roustabouts to pull the trip line from their stern, freeing the anchor so that his own roustabouts could quickly haul it in before it could reengage the bottom. He rang for slow astern and put the wheel to larboard. With the anchor no longer on the bottom, the freshening breeze tried to push the stern of the *Clinton* into the *Kansas City Star*, but the paddlewheel in reverse forced water against the rudders, and the stern stayed put. Pruitt signaled for the mooring crew to let out line, and Benji signaled the crew by pointing both arms at the mooring.

The mooring crew released a lot of slack, and the bow of the *Clinton* started making leeway toward the *Kansas City Star*. Pruitt signaled for the crew to hold, and Benji relayed that signal to the crew. The mooring line went tight, and before the bow had time to come back into line, Pruitt signaled for slack. The *Clinton* continued making sternway out of its berth.

Maneuvering a vessel as large as the *Clinton* is not as straightforward as it may seem. In actual practice, the vessel is not immediately responsive to control inputs and the pilot must anticipate several moves ahead. It's not nearly as easy as driving a coach or sailing a small boat. But Pruitt was more than up to the task this day. As the bow cleared the steamer on either side, the mooring crew had to release the bitter end of the mooring line, and it snaked through the water toward the mooring pole as the motion of the *Clinton* and the hauling of the crew took it around the pole and back to the *Clinton* to be coiled on deck.

Both the *Kansas City Star* and the *Pawnee Chief* blew long salutes with their steam whistles in tribute to the difficulty of the maneuver. Pruitt rang for full ahead, and the *Clinton* was again on her way to the head of navigation of the Missouri River.

Chapter Twelve

Five days later, the *Clinton* backed away from the wharf at St. Joseph. Her next official stop would be Omaha, some one hundred and fifty miles distant. There had been no other mishaps with the vessel and only minor disturbances with the passengers. Danny Barton's face was nearly back to normal, and he and Weedeater had been keeping close track of the potential troublemakers onboard. The McGill and Whitmore brothers had been loud and boisterous in the salon but had shown no tendency toward violence other than conspicuously carrying their weapons.

Robert Pruitt, following his successful extrication from the wharf at Kansas City, had gained confidence as a pilot and was demonstrating a heretofore undisplayed level of competence. In private he had a long discussion with Van Dusen, his engineer, and was endeavoring if not to please Van Dusen at least to irritate him less with overabundant demands for speed and direction changes. He spent most of his off-duty waking hours in the pilothouse, watching and learning from the more-experienced senior pilot, Charles Felden.

The *Barnard Clinton* was running well, maintained in a fine manner by the engineers and the mates. On this part of the river she could make sixty-plus miles in a twenty-four-hour day, and this included one or two stops for wood with other stops for farm products: eggs, beef, pork, vegetables, fruit, and, occasionally, ice.

After the adjustment of watches to accommodate church-goers in Kansas City, Felden now had the midnight watch. This meant that Pruitt had two nighttime watches, eight P.M. and four A.M., but he had handled these with little difficulty these last few days, in part because of the long midsummer days.

Pruitt's best aide to navigation, however, was Felden's exten-sive notebooks. Felden had read the former senior pilot's notes and added them to his own. He had a separate notebook for every section of the river. Pruitt referred to Felden's notes peri-odically during the daylight hours to verify their accuracy and help him interpret Felden's handwriting and abbreviations. But at night, he read every word as he navigated in the darkness, and then, off watch, he copied almost everything into his own expanding notes.

In spite of the relatively trouble-free days, the captain was taking nothing for granted. He observed everything around him, attended every change of watch, requested and received frequent reports from the engineers, conferred with Barton on the behavior of the passengers, and checked the purser's books once and sometimes twice a day. Business as usual.

Pruitt sat up in his bunk. He had been asleep for less than two hours but the late afternoon was too warm for slumber. It was a hot midsummer day. A light breeze was following the *Barnard Clinton*, and it was as if the vessel was stranded in a dead calm, the breeze matching the progress of the steamboat.

Pruitt pulled on his pants and stood in the open doorway of his cabin shirtless and barefoot. That was no help. The setting sun was directly in his face. He decided to finish dressing and descend to the main salon. He put on and buttoned a shirt and tied his tie but left his coat on his bed for the time being. He still had two hours before the change of watch.

All the doors to the main salon were blocked open in hopes of capturing any breeze possible. Inside, the men had all shed their coats, and the women, gathered at the aft end of the salon, were fanning themselves. Dinner was over and the tables had been cleared, so Pruitt went to the bar to see if he could get something cold to drink.

"Mr. Pruitt," the bartender said, "would you like something?"

"Yeah, Skeet. Is there any ice left?"

"No, sir. But the beer is still cold. It won't be tomorrow. How about a bottle of beer?"

"Sure, why not?"

Skeet brought a bottle of cool beer and set it in front of Pruitt, but he didn't linger for conversation. Pruitt quickly drank the beer and then signaled Skeet for another. Skeet brought the second one and again left Pruitt alone to drink it. Pruitt, bored, picked up the bottle and wandered out into the main salon to observe card games.

At one table there were four men playing poker: two Army men, a man in a white shirt, and Harvey Blake. Pruitt watched for a while as one of the Army men raked in a small pot and then the man in the white shirt beckoned Pruitt to fill an empty chair.

"No, thanks," Pruitt declined. "If you don't mind, I'll just watch for a while."

"You're one of the pilots, aren't you?" the white-shirted man asked.

"Yes," Pruitt answered. "I'll have to be in the pilothouse in about an hour."

"Well, you might as well take a load off." He indicated the chair again. Pruitt leaned forward, and seeing this, the man raked a small pile of chips toward that chair. "Here," he said. "Here's a start." Pruitt sat down, and the man began dealing cards for all five players.

Captain Culpepper came in as the headwaiter announced the supper hour. Pruitt looked at his timepiece. It was half past seven in the evening, fifteen minutes before he was to be in the pilothouse. He excused himself, pushed his chips, which had neither grown nor diminished, back to the man in the white shirt, and stood up.

"Thanks for the loan and the hospitality," he said. I have just enough time to get a bite to eat before I return to duty."

"Anytime," the man told him.

The captain was to eat supper again with Abigail Demille, at her invitation. As he entered the main salon, he saw Pruitt push his chips back and stand up. Captain Culpepper didn't approve of gambling, particularly didn't approve of his officers gambling, and he certainly didn't approve of his son, a junior pilot on probation, gambling.

If the captain had seen Pruitt at the table with his drink, he might have felt compelled to take some sort of action. He stopped in his tracks near the exit, knowing that Pruitt would have to walk past him on his way out and to the pilothouse. He said nothing as Pruitt approached but gave him an icy stare as he passed. Pruitt seemed not to notice and continued out of the main salon to report to work in the deepening twilight.

The captain followed him with his eyes and then turned his attention to the table where Miss Demille was waiting for him. He found her interesting; he was sure there was more to her than she let anyone see, and although he respected her reticence, he thought that it wouldn't be a bad thing to know some more about her.

For Abigail it was about the same, although she was far more determined than the captain. After all, she had no apparent responsibilities, no distractions. She could devote her full attention to finding out what she wanted to know. She smiled warmly as he walked to her table and sat down.

"It's very warm tonight, Captain Culpepper," she said.

"Yes," he replied.

"I have seen some of the lower Mississippi steamers that have outside seating for diners."

"Yes. Those are excursion steamers. This is a working

vessel." He was still brooding over seeing Pruitt in the salon, and his answer was quick and flat.

"Oh." She thought he had taken offense and was considering how to retrieve her remark, but he didn't give her time to make amends.

"I must apologize, Miss Demille. I usually leave my concerns for the vessel in the pilothouse."

"Not at all. This is a lovely vessel, and I'm so glad to be here. It was a poor remark. Let's say no more. What should we order for dinner?"

The captain made no reply but studied the menu and after only a minute's consideration beckoned to the waiter.

"And Captain?"

"Yes?"

"Please don't hesitate to tell me anything concerning the operation of the *Barnard Clinton*. I am sincerely interested."

"It's really not very complicated, Miss Demille, uh, Abigail."

The waiter arrived at their table, and they placed their order.

"So, Captain, please tell me about your boat."

"As I said, the mechanics of the boat are quite simple. It's coordinating the work of the crew that requires the most effort."

Abigail's eyes were bright. "How does the engine work, Captain?"

"Steam is the power." He leaned into his conversation slightly. "Now, the steam that comes off a cooking pot may seem light and without force."

"I suppose so."

"But no amount of weight would keep the lid on the pot as long as you keep the water boiling."

"Yes, I'm sure that's true," she said.

"We have four cooking pots; they're called boilers, and they're twenty-six feet long. We inject steam from the boilers into a large tube and that drives the end of the pitman rod one direction, and then we inject steam into the other end of the tube and that drives the pitman rod in the other direction. If you walk to the aft end of the hurricane deck, you can look down on the pitman rods and see how that to-and-fro motion is converted to rotary motion at the paddle wheel."

"I would love to have you show me that after supper."

"I'm afraid it will be too dark by then. Perhaps tomorrow."

"Wonderful. I'm looking forward to it. But tell me, what can go wrong with a machine like that?"

"They wear out."

"Is that dangerous?"

"No."

"What is dangerous?"

"There is little danger on a well-run boat."

"You have a way of making me feel safe." Abigail leaned forward and looked intently into his eyes as she said this. The captain didn't have a reply, but the waiter arrived and made a response unnecessary.

Pruitt arrived in the pilothouse at ten minutes before the hour of eight. This was in conflict with Captain Culpepper's order to begin the change of watch at fifteen minutes before the hour. Felden was surprised at Pruitt's tardiness, but it created no problems since the vessel had been navigating easily all day on this part of the river. The only problem was that Felden could smell alcohol on Pruitt's breath.

"Charles, sorry I'm late. I couldn't get fast service in the dining room."

Felden said nothing and waited until the engineers and the mates had exchanged their information and left. Charles Felden was a direct man. He could tell that Pruitt had been drinking; he could have said something to the effect that it appeared the service was fast enough at the bar, to let Pruitt know of his disapproval. Or he could have ignored the situation, hoping it was a one-time occurrence.

"Mr. Pruitt, you've been drinking. I won't turn over the helm."

Pruitt's face reddened with anger. "I had two glasses of beer with supper." It was actually four glasses, and he had eaten no supper. "I'm quite capable of navigating."

Felden made a quick decision. "All right. I have some chart work to do. I'm going to stay in the pilothouse with you. If you do anything out of line, you'll have to leave, and I'll take over."

Pruitt didn't have a valid argument. "You don't have to do that," was all he could say.

"Captain Culpepper told me you're his son. He also told me that you wouldn't be given another mistake. Don't put me in this position again."

"I understand."

Felden turned his back and began working on his charts.

"Captain, I must say that the food aboard the *Barnard Clinton* is equal to that served in many of the better restaurants in the East."

"I'm pleased that you think so, Miss Demille. I have no basis for judgment in such matters. I can only say that it's better than Army food."

They were finished with supper and could have left, but each of them was hesitant to stand and bring an end to the pleasant interlude.

"As an officer, your meals would have been prepared with more than the usual care."

"In the field I ate with my men."

"That wasn't the standard procedure for men of your rank, was it?"

"It suited me."

"I ate camp fare several times, Captain. It was barely

palatable." It was almost a question; why would anyone make it a regular practice to eat such fare? But the captain had no reply. He had a question of his own.

"What was your role during the war, Abigail?"

Abigail looked at the tabletop as she answered. "I worked in a hospital but sometimes made trips into the field nearer the action."

Captain Culpepper looked closely at Abigail. She was not exactly the fragile type, but he still had trouble seeing her in the vicinity of a battlefield. He had seen corpses with no heads, men torn in half by a cannonball, bloated and rotting bodies, men stacking their dead companions to give themselves cover from which to fire at the enemy and make more death. For this beautiful woman to be in such a setting, or even nearby, was too difficult for him to visualize. He changed the subject.

"Miss DeMille, I believe the stewards are preparing to draw the curtain on the women's quarters." They were sitting in what would shortly be curtained off to give the female salon passengers privacy for the night. "May I walk you back to your cabin?" He rose.

"That would be very nice, Captain." Abigail stood up and took his arm.

Chapter Thirteen

The *Barnard Clinton* was two days from Omaha. It was the change of watch at four in the afternoon. In the pilothouse were the pilots, the mates, the engineers, and the captain. The purser, Jack Galloway, did not often attend the change of watch, being occupied with overseeing food service in the main salon during normal daytime changes at eight A.M., noon, four P.M., and eight P.M. And there was little he could contribute to the operation of the *Clinton*. His duties corresponded to those of a hotel and restaurant manager, and he operated with autonomy. Peter Van Dusen was making a case for a layover.

"The mud drums need to be cleaned out," he said. "We're sanding the boilers."

"For how long?" the captain asked.

"A day and a night," Van Dusen said.

The captain addressed his senior pilot. "Mr. Felden, how is the river compared to two months ago?"

"Down almost two feet according to the marks at the K.C. wharf," Felden answered, and then added, "but the trend is up."

There were normally two periods of high water on the Missouri. The first was during the spring rains on the prairie; the second was due to the snowmelt in the Rocky Mountains. The captain was aware of this phenomenon and was trying to time his two trips per year to the head of navigation to coincide as precisely as possible with high water there.

"That's encouraging," the captain said, "but I have no

information on the amount of snowmelt thus far." The captain looked at the engineer. He knew both of the engineers were competent and accepted what he had been told. "Very well, Mr. Van Dusen. We'll layover twenty-four hours in Omaha. We have a lot of freight for the railroad to unload there, so the additional delay will be minimal. Turn out all hands for the work. After Omaha they can have extra rest. From there, we'll travel only during good light, including moonlight."

"Right," Van Dusen said.

Charles Felden spoke. "While we're cleaning the mud drums, I want the wheel raised six inches. We scheduled it for Sioux City, but given the state of the river, I don't want to wait."

"I'll see to it," senior engineer William Brown said. The captain, by his silence, indicated approval.

The second mate, David Erickson, spoke next. "Mr. Allenby, we have thirty cords of wood onboard, but more than half is cottonwood."

"All right. The east side of the river has several wood hawks over the next twenty miles. We'll try to get some hardwood."

"Mr. Erickson, Mr. Allenby," the captain addressed the two mates, "before we get to Omaha, inventory our liquor and food-stuffs, and whichever of you is on duty when we take on sup-plies, check Mr. Galloway's procurements and reconcile that with the inventory." The two mates nodded with understanding. They had also become suspicious of the new purser.

As the second hand and minute hand came to the top of the pilothouse clock, Robert Pruitt reached from his position at the wheel and rang the bell eight times. Felden stepped up to the wheel to take over the watch.

As the officers started to file out of the pilothouse, the cap-tain asked, "Who has seen Mr. Barton recently?"

Felden answered. "He and Weedeater were up all night watch-ing a high-stakes poker game. Now they're taking turns sleep-ing, and I think you'll find him in his cabin."

While the captain digested this information, Barton walked into the pilothouse, tucking in his shirt. That done, he smoothed his hair and straightened his tie.

"Sorry that I missed the change of watch, Captain." Weedeater had promised to wake him in time for the change of watch but apparently had forgotten. Barton didn't make any excuses.

"Is there trouble brewing in the main salon, Mr. Barton?" the captain asked.

"Maybe. We've been trying to keep the lid on the pot by doubling up in the evening and then catching up on sleep during the day."

"I can't give you any help. The roustabouts are busy preparing to do maintenance at Omaha and rearranging the freight for quick offloading."

"Yes, sir. Could I have Weedeater recruit a couple of reliable roustabouts to come and help us in an emergency?"

"Yes. That's a good idea. But it will have to be a real emergency."

"All right, sir, I'll have him do that before he lies down."

"Where is he sleeping?" The captain realized that Weedeater had no official standing and was likely still sleeping with the other roustabouts. But that wasn't the case.

"I'm sharing my cabin. He wouldn't be able to sleep on deck or in the main salon during the day," Barton answered.

"Very well. Make sure he has a key to the gun cabinet."

"Yes, sir."

"Mr. Barton, we must not have our passengers endangered. If we have to put someone off for you to keep the peace, that's what we'll do."

As if on cue, gunfire was heard coming from the main salon.

The gamblers who had kept Barton and Weedeater on edge all night had decided not to wait until evening to resume their game. The losers wanted to reverse their losses; the winners, thinking they were on a winning streak, wanted to make more gains. They had started gambling right after the midday meal, short of rest, and short of patience.

The men at the table were the gambler, a large man named Nelson Carner, one Army officer named Major Williams, two of the Whitmore brothers, and Donald McGill. Peter McGill and Gary Whitmore had been watching over their respective brothers' shoulders.

The major was smart. He had been able to win modestly during the previous night. The Whitmores and McGill had not been smart. They had gambled away several hundred dollars—most of their savings—and were determined to win it back. The big winner, naturally, was Carner.

The game had started a little after three, and after four hands the Whitmores had lost the rest of their cash. When Carner refused to give them credit, they became belligerent. Carner, realizing that there was no more money to be won from these brothers, wanted to extricate himself from the scene and let the brothers cool down. Too late.

"Sit down, Carner, you ain't goin' nowhere with our money!" Harold Whitmore exploded.

Carner was half out of his chair and he eased himself back down, realizing that defiance at this moment could cost him. But neither did he allow himself to appear intimidated by the rough men angrily facing him.

"Gentlemen, if you have more money, or anything of value, I would be happy to continue playing cards and give you every opportunity to win." He picked up the deck and shuffled it without looking as he watched the men's eyes.

"I got a Colt Army .44," John Whitmore said, and pulled it from his belt by the grip. Carner took his right hand off the deck he had been shuffling.

"Let me see it," Carner requested, ignoring the ominous implication.

John Whitmore pulled the hammer back and pushed the barrel toward Carner's face. "Can you see it?" he asked loudly.

The major, having served in the Union Army since the beginning of the war, didn't want to see violence erupt in what had been a peaceful setting until now. "Take it easy, there, mister. It's only a card game. I'll stake you to a couple of hands."

"The day I let some blue belly give me or mine a handout is never gonna happen!" Harold Whitmore said and drew his own gun.

Weedeater had not been far from the table, but he was on the side facing the belligerent brothers. He tried to circle the table to get behind them, but Gary Whitmore, who had not been taking part in the gambling, stepped in front of him. Weedeater put him down with a quick swing of the butt of his shotgun. Seeing that, John Whitmore turned his gun on Weedeater and shot him in the shoulder. Weedeater dropped his shotgun and went to one knee, both from pain and in an effort to pick up his weapon. Major Williams pushed back from the table, pulling his own revolver awkwardly from its cavalry-style holster, and Harold Whitmore shot him in the chest. Williams went to the floor. A derringer appeared in Carner's hand and he shot John Whitmore in the head, killing him instantly. Then Carner dived under the table as Harold and Gary Whitmore both fired their pistols at him, missing.

It was at this moment that Danny Barton entered the main salon from the front entrance. He could tell by the heavy sulphur smell and the thick cloud of gun smoke hanging over the gambling table where the action was taking place, but as he tried to make his way down the hall between the kitchen and the purser's office, escaping passengers slowed him down. There were several more shots as the Whitmore brothers, and Mc-Gill fired at anything that moved in the salon. Then they ran to a side exit.

Seeing the men run to the exit, Barton reversed his path and went out and around the main salon on the side deck. There he saw the two McGill brothers and the two remaining Whitmore brothers climbing the aft staircase to the hurricane deck. He shouted to them to stop, and they turned and fired at him. He got off one shot, and Peter McGill jumped over the railing into the Missouri River. Now there were three gunmen left, and they climbed to the hurricane deck.

There were two yawls on the hurricane deck. One was suspended from davits, ready to launch for those who knew how to handle the winches. The other was in blocks on the deck. As Barton ran back up the forward stairs, the three men slid the yawl off its blocks and pushed it over the side. Firing one more time as Barton's head appeared, they jumped into the river.

The security officer ran to the hurricane deck, with gun in hand, but the men were hanging on to the far side of the yawl, and he had no chance for an effective shot. Nevertheless, he emptied his revolver into the yawl, hoping at least to sink her and deny the men their escape. With the steamer making headway upstream and the current taking the yawl away, they were soon out of range of his revolver.

Chapter Fourteen

The scene in the main salon was grim. Weedeater had been shot twice but was still conscious and sitting up. Carner had been hit three times with bullets that penetrated the top of the gambling table under which he had hidden. His wounds were more uncomfortable than lethal, the wooden top having taken much of the energy out of the lead missiles. Major Williams was lying in a pool of blood, unconscious; John Whitmore, also in a pool of blood, was dead. Skeet, the bartender, and two male passengers had wounds that appeared not as serious.

Abigail Demille, who had been in her cabin when the shooting started, grabbed her medical bag and hurried to the main salon, following the captain as he exited the pilothouse. Culpepper restrained her from entering the salon until he made sure that the shooting was over, and then let her rush to the side of Major Williams. Moving rapidly and skillfully, she cut his shirt away to expose his wound. She placed a handful of gauze over the hole in his chest and directed an onlooker to hold it in place firmly. Then she went to John Whitmore and quickly determined that there was nothing she could do for him.

Weedeater filled the captain in on what had taken place. "Cap'n, they lost a lotta money last night and I reckon they decided to get even with gunpowder instead'a cards."

"Who shot the major?"

"One'a the Whitmores that ran outta here." Weedeater was unaware that the outlaws had left the boat. He was still holding his shotgun tightly with his good arm in case they returned to the main salon.

Captain Culpepper beckoned Abigail to Weedeater's side. Weedeater had a hole in his left shoulder and was missing a piece of his ear where a bullet had only just missed his head. He would have gotten to his feet if the captain hadn't held him down.

"Miss Demille, see to the major, please," the captain said. "I'll take care of this man. The others don't appear to be in dire circumstances."

Abigail wordlessly went to the major's side and began trying to save his life. Danny entered the main salon and found the captain.

"Captain, those four men stole our extra yawl and have gone downriver."

The captain wasted no words. "Take four roustabouts. Find them and kill them. Bring our yawl back. We'll wait for you in Omaha."

The tone of his voice let Danny know there was no room for discussion on the matter. Danny left the main salon on the run to find the needed roustabouts on the cargo deck. From there they went to the hurricane deck, stopping at Danny's cabin to get rifles and ammunition, then to the yawl, which they expertly lowered into the water. Two enlisted men came to them as they were boarding the yawl.

"We want to come along," one of them said. Danny looked at the two men, wondering if they would be an asset or a liability. "We liked the major. He treated us right." They both had revolvers but no rifles. The four rifles Danny had taken from the gun cabinet would be enough, he decided.

"Can you handle a Henry?" he asked.

"Like a baby," the second one said.

"All right, get in and load up these rifles."

In minutes all six men were pulling hard on the oars with

Danny on the tiller. They sped downstream in determined pursuit.

Abigail knew that the major was staying in the captain's cabin. When she had done as much as she could do for him, she directed two enlisted men to carry him carefully to his bed and to stay with him until she arrived. Then she turned her attention to the other wounded.

"Mr. Weedeater, let me see your arm." She gently picked up his forearm to see that the bullet had gone cleanly through his upper arm without breaking the bone.

The maid, Eleanor, came to Abigail's side. "Miss Abigail, can I he'p?" she asked.

"Bless your heart, Eleanor, yes, you can. Clean this man's arm and his ear. Bandage his arm, but leave his ear uncovered so I can stitch it. Then find me, because I'll probably need help with the others."

"Yes, ma'am," Eleanor said.

"Mr. Weedeater, you stay right here and whatever Eleanor tells you to do, you do." Abigail looked at Eleanor's face in time to see a trace of a smile. She left the two of them and went to the gambler, Nelson Carner.

Abigail had met Carner, as she had met all the male passengers, weeks ago. Carner was laying on his stomach, in pain and groaning with every breath.

"Mr. Carner, where are you hurt?"

"I got hit in the back. More than once I think."

"Hit? Do you mean shot?"

"Yes. Shot. Definitely shot," he groaned.

Abigail used a small knife to cut the seam up the back of the gambler's coat. Then she cut his shirt to expose his back. Most of the flesh on his back was discolored by bruising. There was a hole on his right shoulder blade, one a little lower, and one on his right buttock. She could see the bullets and splinters of wood in the top two holes; they hadn't penetrated his shoulder blade.

"Did you just ruin my hundred-dollar jacket?" Carner asked through clenched teeth, as he tried to turn his head around far enough to see her.

"No, Mr. Carner, but I did cut your shirt. They can both be resewn. Now hold still."

When Abigail was finished with Carner, she next went to Skeet, who had only a laceration in his side. The two wounded passengers likewise had only minor injuries. She returned to Weedeater and began stitching his ear.

The captain had taken the shotgun from Weedeater and had followed Abigail from patient to patient, watching her occasionally, but mainly watching everyone in the room with eyes as sharp as an eagle's. When Abigail had finished with Weedeater, he struggled to his feet and addressed the captain.

"I'll take that shotgun, now, Cap'n. With Danny down the river, I'm gonna be doin' his part and mine."

The captain looked at Weedeater, and something in the rough roustabout's face told him that the man would handle his additional responsibilities or die in the attempt.

"Very well, Mr. Koslosky." He handed the shotgun to Weedeater and added, "Find another roustabout to help you, and I'll get him a gun."

"Yes, sir," Weedeater replied, surprised that anyone knew his real name. He walked to the exit, turned once to survey the room, and then went out to find a helper.

"Miss DeMille, we have used your skills twice. I am again impressed."

"Thank you, Captain. Now I want to go to the major. His wound is more serious." She turned to Eleanor. "You come with me, Eleanor."

"Sho', Miss Abigail. I carry yo' bag."

"That would be fine, Eleanor, thank you."

Abigail walked toward the exit, followed by Eleanor looking quite proud but serious, and then Captain Culpepper. When they reached the Texas deck Abigail and Eleanor went to the captain's cabin. The captain went to Barton's cabin and took a repeating rifle and a box of cartridges from the cabinet. Then he went to the pilothouse.

Felden, Pruitt, and Pruitt's mate, Erickson, were still in the pilothouse. Both pilots also had keys to the gun cabinet, and they had taken one rifle for themselves, to be kept in the pilothouse until further notice. The captain saw the rifle standing in the corner when he entered.

"That's good," he said.

"What happened, Captain?" Pruitt asked. Felden never took his attention from the river. The sun was setting.

"The Whitmores and the McGills started a gunfight. They took our yawl." The crew in the pilothouse had witnessed this. The captain continued. "I sent Mr. Barton after them."

"Was anyone killed?" Felden asked without turning.

"One of the Whitmores," the captain said. "And Major Williams is critically wounded."

"Is Danny going to try to bring them back?" Erickson asked.

"No."

There was a short silence as each man reached the same conclusion on his own. The captain had told Barton how he wanted the outlaws handled, and it didn't include taking them anywhere.

"The roustabout, Weedeater, was also wounded but not seriously. He's going to act in Mr. Barton's place until Barton returns," the captain said. "This rifle is for the roustabout he chooses to help him. I'll just leave it here until he comes for it." He stood the rifle next to the pilothouse rifle.

"We'll see he gets it," Pruitt said.

"Very well. I want to check on Major Williams now."

Captain Culpepper left the pilothouse and walked to his cabin. When he arrived at the door, it was standing open. Inside, Abigail, Eleanor, and the two roustabouts who had carried the injured officer to his cabin were all standing with heads hung low. Abigail looked up as the captain's frame filled the open doorway.

"The major died, Captain," Abigail said sadly.

"I see."

"It would have been a miracle if he had survived his wound."

The captain seemed to be organizing his thoughts. After a moment, he said, "I had several conversations with Major Williams. He was wounded three times during the war; he had his horse shot from under him twice, once by a cannonball that tore the animal in half. He sidestepped death five times while doing his duty in preserving the union. To die like this is . . ." The captain didn't finish. He stood in silence for several minutes, then spoke quietly to the two roustabouts. "Thank you for your efforts, men. We're shorthanded right now. Report to the mate for duty."

"Yes, sir," one said, and they left the Texas deck to work on the main deck.

"Eleanor, you should get back to your regular duties also. Thank you for your help."

Abigail added, "Yes, Eleanor, thank you." She took the maid's hand in hers and then let it go. Eleanor left, leaving only the captain and Abigail standing over the dead major. At length, the captain broke the silence.

"Are you all right, Abigail?"

"Oh, quite. I am not unused to things like this. Are *you* all right?"

"Miss DeMille, I, like Major Williams, was at Antietam in 1862. I won't soon forget the date, September 17."

"That has become known as the bloodiest day of the war," Abigail said, speaking even more quietly than the captain.

"Just so. But we continued to prosecute the war as if it meant nothing."

"The war has been over more than a year now," she mused.

"Nevertheless, it seems, the killing goes on."

Abigail took the captain's hand in hers. "Come on," she said. "Let's sit out here." The captain followed her out of the room, closing the door behind them and following her to the hurricane deck, where they sat on the blocks that had cradled the stolen yawl. They sat in silence as the sun disappeared and the sky turned dark.

Chapter Fifteen

The four outlaws had managed to find only two oars when they pushed the yawl off the hurricane deck. Not knowing how to row a boat, they were using these awkwardly as paddles. The current, however, took them rapidly away from the *Barnard Clinton*. By the time Barton and his crew of four roustabouts and two soldiers launched the regular yawl, the outlaws were out of sight.

The four roustabouts were experienced oarsmen. The two soldiers were not, but they positioned themselves between the pairs of roustabouts and soon were rowing well enough to make a contribution to the progress downstream. They all knew that the outlaws had at least twenty minutes' head start on them, and the sun would be setting in less than an hour.

As they rounded each bend, Danny would strain to see downriver, first the water catching the last light from a fading sky, then both banks for any sign of the stolen yawl. They might have left it carelessly tied to a bush at the water's edge, or they might have pulled it completely up the banks or onto a sandbar. He left nothing unexamined. He also knew that they could be waiting in ambush somewhere. He remembered that they had rifles. The river was not wide on this stretch; a good rifleman could shoot across its full width and hit a man.

Danny had brought lanterns, but he knew they were not bright enough to illuminate the shoreline; they were only bright enough to make his crew a good target. He chose not to light them. They continued downriver, all eyes on both banks, aware of how vulnerable they were. Something splashed along the western bank and two roustabouts dropped their oars and grabbed their rifles. One oar stayed in its lock and the other slipped through. Danny put the tiller hard over so that he could retrieve it.

"It's all right men. It was probably only a beaver," he reassured them as he handed the oar back to the nervous roustabout. The two soldiers, having experienced many patrols in enemy territory, were less excitable and continued pulling on their oars. As if to verify Danny's statement, a beaver swam by the stern, curious about this piece of driftwood that had a voice.

As the last of the light faded, Danny wondered what he should do next. If the outlaws stayed on the river, they would eventually be overtaken, but in the dark. If they pulled out somewhere to spend the night, Danny and his crew would pass them right by. Considering these two possibilities, Danny thought he had a proper course of action. He would slow the yawl down to conserve the men's strength, but continue downriver. If they passed the outlaws in the night, it would not matter; he presumed that the outlaws would only travel with the current, having neither the equipment, the desire, nor the ability to go upriver. If they didn't overtake the outlaws during the night, they would at least be closer. He was about to verbalize this to his crew when one of them spoke.

"Mr. Barton." He was almost whispering. "I smell woodsmoke. And something cooking."

Barton took in a deep breath. "Yeah, so do I," he responded in the same whisper. Now his strategy could be changed. "Lift your oars and let her drift." The wind was from the west. "We'll drift down about five hundred yards, then as quietly as we can, we'll pull into the west bank."

The crew followed his instructions and when they had gone

about five hundred yards, Danny said, "All right, make for the shore." They could barely make out the silhouette of the western side of the river against the starlit sky, but they pulled gently on the oars as Barton swung the tiller. In minutes they felt the keel of the yawl slide across the bottom at the edge of the river.

Danny addressed the men. "Humpback, you and Little Bit stay here with two rifles. Keep alert. If you hear someone coming, take the yawl out into the river. When we come back, I'll give you a low whistle so you'll know it's us." He then touched each of the other men on the shoulder. "Follow me as quietly as you can."

Barton thought that the woodsmoke was coming from a homesteader's cabin. It was likely, he surmised, that the outlaws had stopped here for the night, knowing they could get food, perhaps steal some horses, and at the very least be off the river for the night.

Danny, the two soldiers, and the two other roustabouts slowly walked through the ankle-deep water and found the shore. It was a struggle for them to climb the bank quietly in the dark, but once they gained the top, there was just grass with occasional trees and low bushes. They could tell that the river was on their right, more by sound than sight, and they continued along the top of the bank until they saw a light in the window of a cabin. They couldn't tell the size of the cabin or whether there were outbuildings or fences, but they continued forward until they were within a hundred yards of the lighted window. Danny stopped them.

"You men stay right here. I'm going in for a closer look."

"Look," said one soldier and pointed across the river where the first piece of the nearly full moon was showing above the horizon.

"Good," Danny whispered, and he began making his way toward the cabin. He had a brief doubt about how he had proceeded since leaving the river. There were two men at the river with the yawl, which was the only means of regaining the *Clinton*; there were four men standing in a pasture in the dark, and he, armed with only a revolver that he hoped was still dry, was approaching a cabin that might be full of dangerous men. The brief moment of doubt passed, and he continued toward the cabin.

If the men were indeed in the cabin, they couldn't have been there more than a few minutes. They probably wouldn't be expecting a contingent from the steamer. Danny was close enough now to hear voices from within the cabin. Some sounded angry. He was almost to the front door when it opened and one of the outlaws stepped out to see him in the light from the rising moon. In spite of the dim light from a lamp in the cabin, the man's eyes took just a few seconds to adjust to the moonlight. Time enough for Danny to recognize Harold Whitmore.

"Who the devil are you?" the man shouted as he pulled his pistol from his belt.

Danny already had his gun in his hand and shot the man in his chest. The man's gun discharged into the air, and he fell back against the cabin, dead.

Peter McGill came to the door, gun in hand, and Danny shot him in the chest. The man didn't go down, however, and leveled his gun at Danny. Danny shot him in the head, and he fell back into the cabin.

Danny quickly stepped up to the door and entered the cabin, gun in hand. There he stood face to face with Donald McGill, who was holding a shotgun aimed at Danny's waist. Danny's first shot hit the man in his left forearm. He released his grip on the forestock of the shotgun and the weight of the two barrels pulled the weapon off its aim. He pulled the trigger, and the dirt floor in front of Danny erupted in dust and lead pellets. Danny's second shot hit McGill in the chest as he was trying to raise the barrels of the gun with just his right hand.

The gun fell to the floor. McGill tried to get his revolver out of his belt as he stood on unsteady legs. Danny had shot five times; he never carried his pistol with a loaded chamber under the hammer, and the gun was now empty. He hoped the two remaining outlaws didn't guess this. McGill slowly sagged to the floor and fell face forward. There were just Danny, Gary Whitmore, and the family who lived in the cabin.

Whitmore had a woman by her hair and was holding her in front of himself as a shield. In his right hand was a single-shot muzzle-loading pistol. Danny pulled the hammer back on his empty pistol and brought it up to eye level, aiming carefully at Whitmore's head.

"Looks like we each got just one shot, kid," the man grinned. "You're gonna eat mine, and all you got to shoot at is this here woman." He pulled the hammer back on the pistol.

The two soldiers and two roustabouts that Danny had left at the edge of the yard came running at the first sound of gunfire. One of the soldiers burst into the room, startling Whitmore, who swung his gun toward the soldier. Danny rushed across the narrow space separating them in the small cabin and he, the woman, and Whitmore all crashed to the floor as Whitmore's gun discharged into the ceiling. The woman wriggled away and escaped.

Whitmore was an Indian fighter who knew a lot of tricks of close combat. Danny was young and strong, but he was not a match for the fighting skill of Gary Whitmore. As they wrestled with each other, Whitmore got the advantage and soon had Danny under him with his hands on Danny's throat. It would have ended there but for the soldier who stepped forward and put the barrel of his revolver against Whitmore's head.

"Let 'im go, buddy," he said.

"Go to blazes!" Whitmore replied.

The soldier shot Whitmore in the head at point-blank range. It was over.

Danny pushed the lifeless body to one side as he tried to get air back into his lungs. The soldier, Sergeant Brown, glanced around the room and, seeing only a frightened homestead family, helped Danny sit up.

"You all right, Barton?"

"Yeah, Sarge, thanks. You got here just in time."

"Well, it looks like you did most of the work. All four of those outlaws are dead. Well done."

Danny looked around the room from where he sat on the dirt floor. "How are the people who live here?"

The sergeant looked around and saw a young boy, a baby in a crib, and a woman, all huddled in a corner of the room. There was a man lying face up on the floor, a knife in his chest.

"I guess one of 'em didn't make it. Is that your husband, ma'am?" he asked the woman. She didn't answer. The sergeant helped Danny to his feet as the rest of Danny's crew entered the cabin.

"Drag the outlaws out to the woods," said Danny. He looked around the cabin. It was obvious that this family had almost nothing in the way of possessions. There were two log platforms piled with straw that served as beds. Only one of them had a blanket. The baby's crib was also made from large sticks tied with leather. A rock hearth with a wooden chimney suspended above was for their heat and cold-weather cooking. A shelf on one wall held their meager foodstuffs and two carved wooden spoons. Flat rocks had apparently served as plates. The only window was just an opening in one wall that could be covered with cloth or leather in cold weather. Because of the scarcity of belongings, Danny felt sure that this family had only been here since spring. He went to the woman, who was still clutching the young boy.

"Is that your husband, ma'am?" he said repeating the sergeant's question.

She looked at him with eyes wide and finally found her

voice. "He brought me here after my man died. This boy is his. The young'un is mine."

"I'm sorry about what happened. Is it all right if we take him outside? We'll bury him before we leave."

"I can't stay here," she said.

"Where can you go?"

"Me and these two kids are gonna go with you. We don't own this place. We just moved in. There ain't nothing for us here without a man."

"I don't know if we can do that," Danny said.

"Might just as well bury us too, then," she said.

Danny estimated her to be no older than eighteen. The man that he had thought was her husband looked a lot older. They were both small in stature, and she was as thin as a sapling. She was wearing a loose-fitting dress that was mended and patched in several spots but, as far as Danny could see in the dim light, was clean. She was missing one of her front teeth and her nose was off center. Her eyes seemed much older than her face and spoke of hard labor and relentless discomfort. The only person in the group with shoes was the dead man. There was no rifle or shotgun visible in the cabin and outside he had seen no signs of livestock. He realized that she had correctly appraised her situation.

"All right. We'll bury your man tonight, and then we'll start back up the river. If you have any food, we'd sure like some supper."

"The boy brought back a possum and two rabbits today. I'll get 'em a'cookin' out back." She faced the boy. "Go get that fire a'goin' and then fetch me some water, Isaac. We got comp'ny for supper." The woman, over her fear now, was as matter-of-fact as if nothing had taken place in the little cabin that had been her temporary home.

After they had eaten, they buried the dead men. Then they stood on the bank that looked down on the Missouri.

Danny spoke. "Isaac, would you like to say something in memory of your father?" Isaac didn't speak, didn't shake or nod his head. He stood motionless, staring at the water flowing past.

"His name was Carl White," the young woman said.

"All right," Danny said. He clasped his hands in front of himself and lowered his head slightly. "Lord," he said, "we're sending you one of your soldiers. He didn't get his full measure on earth. Maybe you can make up for that when he gets there. Please make Carl White welcome." He said amen, and the others, except for Isaac, repeated that.

"Men," Danny said, "all these men had of value was their guns—two pistols and two long guns. Does anyone want to keep them?"

"I ain't ready to take hardware from dead men," one of the roustabouts said.

"No," said the others, and the sergeant added, "They didn't have much luck with 'em."

Danny picked up one of the pistols and threw it into the muddy waters below. Then the other pistol and both long guns. "Let's see if we can find the other yawl."

Chapter Sixteen

The next day passed quietly on the *Barnard Clinton*. Captain Culpepper, as usual, spent most of his time in the pilothouse, but occasionally he would take his binoculars to the hurricane deck and scan the river behind them. Only when the sun set would he leave the Texas deck and descend to the main salon. Because of the upset of the gunfight and the death of the major, he thought it was more important than ever to dine with the passengers, no matter how unpleasant he sometimes found their conversation.

"Captain, I was hoping there would be some musicians onboard for entertainment." The speaker was a salesman who had boarded at St. Joseph.

The captain forced a smile. "It's more profitable to carry cargo."

"Perhaps so," the man persisted, "but you know, music is something that would not work well on the trains. Because of the noise, you know. Yet people desire to be entertained during the long days of transit across this godforsaken country. If steamboats are to survive, they must provide a service unique to their abilities."

"I'll discuss your idea with the owners," the captain said.

"And well you should. The railroads are going to make life difficult for riverboats. You could have the first riverboat on the Missouri to provide music." Then the man had another idea.

"Perhaps even dancing girls, eh?" He looked around the table to see if his suggestion had been appreciated by any of the other men.

The captain was rescued by another male diner who changed the subject. "Captain, is it true that we'll be in Omaha tomorrow?"

"Yes, that is our objective."

"What time will we arrive? Will we be able to disembark immediately?"

"We should be there midday. I can't be more specific than that. We've found the river to be different than it was only two months ago. And yes, as soon as we touch the wharf, the stages will go down, and passenger loading and unloading will get the highest priority."

"But I understand you have a considerable amount of freight for Omaha. Won't you want to start unloading at the first opportunity?"

"Yes. We'll use the starboard stage for offloading freight. The passengers and the small amount of incoming freight will use the larboard stage. I ask you to be careful disembarking."

"Larboard?"

"Left. Starboard is right. As you face forward on the vessel."

A well-dressed woman spoke. "Captain. I've noticed that both our small boats are gone. If we had to abandon ship, how would we be able to survive?"

"There are floats positioned around the outside of the vessel for those who can't swim. And there are few places on the Missouri where a boat this size would be able to sink below the Texas deck. Our problem is usually not having enough depth."

"But, Captain . . ."

"Now, Flora," the woman beside her interrupted, "you just like to worry." She turned toward the captain. "How big is Omaha, Captain?"

"It is growing so rapidly that no one actually knows. If one counts the soldiers, the railroad workers, the Indians, and the travelers, it might be ten thousand."

The woman put her hand to her throat. "Oh, my, there are Indians in Omaha?"

"Yes."

"Oh. Oh my. I was told there were no Indians in eastern Nebraska." The woman was distressed.

"I wouldn't worry too much, Mrs. Carruthers. The Indians in eastern Nebraska are generally well behaved."

The man who opened the conversation asked, "Didn't the government give the Indians a lot of land somewhere else? Why aren't they all there?"

The captain did not betray his contempt for the ignorance of the man's statement. He merely said, "The Pawnee who used to live here were 'relocated' to the Indian territory about thirty years ago. There are still some Pawnee around who farm and sell wood along the river. They get along well with the white man."

"Captain, I've heard stories of Indian attacks all along the upper Platte River."

"Those are stories told by white men who would like the Army to eliminate the Indians."

"But you said that the Indians had been moved to Oklahoma."

"The Pawnee. Some Sioux tribes have moved onto the former Pawnee lands. They are annoyances, nothing more."

Abigail thought the captain was losing patience with this subject. She rescued him. "Captain, how long will we be in Omaha?"

"We'll be there at least twenty-four hours. The yawl is on an errand downstream, and we'll await its return. It shouldn't take long."

"Will we also see Council Bluffs?"

"No. There are ferries that make that trip." Although the *Clinton* had visited Council Bluffs in the spring, the captain was now anxious to have few delays. The farther upriver he could deliver the Army freight, the higher his profit would be.

"So, we will be in the Dakota Territory in just a few days. Is that right, Captain?" It was Flora.

"Yes. Would you excuse me now? I want to be present in the pilothouse when the watch changes." The captain pushed back from the table. He had not had a chance to eat much of his meal, but it was cold now, and he legitimately wanted to observe the watch change. He bowed quickly to the passengers sitting at the table, and then he walked to the exit.

Abigail noted the time. It was twenty minutes before the hour of four P.M. That would give her just enough time to finish her own meal, go to her cabin to freshen up, and then see if she could extricate the captain from the pilothouse.

Chapter Seventeen

Harvey Blake leaned casually on the counter that separated the purser's office from the rest of the main salon. He had been absent during the gunfight in the salon and now wanted to find out what had happened and whether or not it would interfere with his plans.

"Who started the fight?" he asked.

"One of the Whitmore brothers. None of 'em were very smart," Purser Jack Galloway said.

"And they killed the Army man and the two guards?"

"No, just the major. The guard they call Weedeater was shot up a little, but not too bad." Galloway nodded his head toward Weedeater, who was making his way through the salon.

"How about the other guard?"

"That kid? He and some other men took the yawl down the river after the Whitmores and McGills. We'll never see them again." Galloway was contemptuous of Danny Barton and the attempt to catch the outlaws.

"Can you be sure?"

"Think about it. They headed downstream just before dark. The current here is better than five miles per hour; the boat is making three miles per hour over the bottom. They'd have to row eight miles per hour just to keep pace." Galloway watched Blake's face to see if he could understand the simple mathematics. "And they're probably ten miles below us. All they can do is wait for the *Clinton* to come back down three weeks from now. If the Whitmores don't kill them all, which is good odds."

"I'm thinking we should do what we have to do right now. The boat is shorthanded, and this is the last night before Omaha. Tonight might be our best opportunity. I've found out that we might not travel after dark beyond Omaha."

"Did you have something in mind?"

"Yeah, a boiler explosion," Blake answered.

"How will you do that?"

"Tie the safety valves down." Blake had only a rudimentary idea of the operation of a steamboat.

"That won't work," the purser said, shaking his head.

"Why not?" Blake snapped. "Boiler explosions happen on the Mississippi every year. I saw the remains of one a day later. There wasn't enough left to salvage."

"The boilers are just inside the main entrance to the cargo bay. There's always work going on there, even at night. And tying the popoffs down won't guarantee an explosion. We're burning mostly cottonwood now, and it's hard enough just to get the boilers up to normal operating pressure."

Blake was becoming irritated with Galloway. "I can make them blow up. You just say when."

"What are you going to do?"

"Don't worry about it. I'll get it done."

"It'll have to be after Omaha or we might not get the rest of our money," Galloway said, barely concealing his irritation.

"I'll get it done," Blake repeated, and walked away from the office to watch the gambling.

Abigail stepped out of her cabin and walked along the Texas deck to the pilothouse. It wouldn't be bad, she thought, if she and the captain could sit out on the blocks on the hurricane deck and watch the stars as they did the previous night. They had talked little that night, and then had bid each other good night and gone to their respective cabins. If she could repeat that setting, perhaps she could get more conversation from the captain. She was fascinated by him and thought perhaps he had become somewhat taken with her. His habitually stern, military manner made it difficult for her to know what he was thinking.

The summer nights had become quite warm, and the doors to the pilothouse were standing open as Abigail climbed the half stairs and stepped inside. Charles Felden was at the wheel, but the captain was not there.

"Oh, excuse me. Mr. Felden, isn't it?"

"Yes, Miss Demille." After a quick glance over his shoulder, he returned his attention to the river.

"I was looking for Captain Culpepper."

"He's doing bookwork in his cabin. First one behind the pilothouse, same side as yours."

"Thank you, Mr. Felden." Abigail stepped out and descended the half stairs to the first cabin. She tapped lightly on the door.

"Yes?" The captain's voice came through the door.

"It's Abigail, Captain Culpepper," she said.

"One moment."

Abigail stood at the rail as she waited for the captain to come to the door. The soft, deep *whomp*, *whomp*, *whomp* of the steam engines drowned out the night sounds of the river except for a coyote that must have been at the top of the bank looking right down at the *Barnard Clinton*. As the *Clinton* swung in tight to the eastern bank, an owl asked his age-old question from the top of a tree: *Whoooo* was this strange contraption making its way up his river in the dark? An answering *whooo* came from another tree farther upstream. The captain opened his door.

"Good evening, Abigail."

"Am I interrupting your work, Captain?" In spite of the fact that she had persuaded him to call her Abigail, she still could not bring herself to call him by his first name, and he hadn't requested it.

"No, I believe I found out what I wanted to find out."

Abigail tilted her head in an unspoken question.

"It's a business matter I'll have to attend to before we reach Omaha."

"Nothing unpleasant, I hope," she said.

"Just business," he said, but she thought that his face betrayed that the "business" was distasteful. She changed the subject.

"I think I'd like to sit on the yawl blocks and enjoy this warm evening. Would you care to join me?"

"Yes," he said. He closed and locked the door to his cabin. "If you'd like, I'll have the steward bring us some lemonade."

"Oh, how nice," she said.

The night was warm and calm. The speed of the *Clinton* through the water had the effect of a three-mile-per-hour breeze—just enough to take the insects of the night away. The two of them were comfortable with the night and with each other. Neither felt the need to fill the night with conversation. They sipped their lemonades and only occasionally broke the silence, silence being a relative term, as the engines maintained their pulsing moan.

"It's almost like a heartbeat, isn't it?"

"You wouldn't be the first to compare a riverboat to a living organism."

"Do you love her? The boat?" she asked.

"I respect her."

"Ah." She raised her glass and took a drink. The *Clinton* had been following the eastern bank in a sweeping left turn and now had to make a crossing to the western bank as the river changed course. There was a leadsman on the bow, and they could hear him calling out depths to the pilothouse. They could feel, rather than see, the boat turning to starboard as the pilot found the western bank and the channel. Soon the leads-man stopped calling.

"Your pilots seem to have exceptional eyesight in the dark."

"I'm not sure they rely on their eyesight."

"You mean they have the ability to sense the shallows and the sides of the river?"

"I just know that they don't always need to see."

Abigail considered this statement for a moment. "I suppose they're well compensated?"

"The pilot is the highest paid person on the vessel," he replied, "but all the officers receive satisfactory salaries."

The obvious next question would inquire about the captain's own earnings, but Abigail was too polite for that. Instead, she said, "It also appears to me that you treat your personnel very well."

"Oh?" The captain had not reflected a great deal on what would be the proper treatment for his workers. He had a natural ability to inspire confidence and loyalty. "I have little tolerance for laziness in action or thought. My crew, with a few exceptions, seldom tests my patience in these areas. I respect them as much as I respect the boat."

"And it certainly appears they respect you in return."

The captain made no reply and the two of them sat quietly for some time. Now it was Abigail who was reticent. She thought it might be time to reveal more of herself to the captain, but on the other hand, she wondered why he had never questioned her about her past. In the end she decided to wait for a better time.

"Captain, I believe I'd like to retire now."

Captain Culpepper stood and then extended his hand to Abigail to help her to her feet, but she didn't release his hand when she stood. She pressed their clenched hands to her throat and looked into his eyes. There was only the light from a deck lamp, and she could not see his face. She released his hand.

He put it gently against her back as he walked her across the hurricane deck to her cabin and bid her good night.

Twenty miles to the south, Danny Barton, the four roustabouts, the two soldiers, the woman, Fern was her name, her baby, and the orphaned Isaac were making their way up the river. They had rowed all night and all day, towing the other yawl, but had not gained on the *Clinton,* although they had no way of knowing this.

"How are you men doing?" Danny asked the roustabouts, whose pulling on the oars was less powerful than it had been.

"Mr. Barton," one of the roustabouts said between strokes, "either this water's gettin' thicker, or my oar's gettin' heavier."

"It's an hour before midnight," Danny said. "Can you keep going until daylight?"

"If that's what you want, I reckon."

Danny made a quick decision. Besides the fact that the men were less able to fight the current upstream than earlier, the boat, in the darkness, was also not taking the easiest route upriver, wasting time and effort. They had just passed the Platte River and that meant they were within twenty-five miles of Omaha. The current on this part of the Missouri averaged five miles per hour, almost as much as they could accomplish with oars. But if they kept going, he was afraid they would slowly lose the ability to overcome the flow.

"No," he said. "Let's find a place to spend the night."

The sergeant expressed his doubts. "How will we catch the boat if we stop. They're going to travel all night."

"They're going to stop at Omaha for twenty-four hours midday tomorrow. We'll find them there."

"We're alongside a sandbar now, Mr. Barton. That might be the safest place."

"All right, I'm swinging her in." Danny put the tiller over and in minutes the yawl scraped into the sandbar. A roustabout jumped out with the painter in hand and began pulling. The others followed suit and soon both yawls were high and dry next to a group of bushes and tied up.

"Isaac," Fern ordered, as she stood, cradling her baby in her arms, "get us a fire goin' t'other side a' them bushes. It's gonna get cold before light." The boy began picking up sticks without a word. He had yet to speak to anyone. "That boy sure knows how to make fire," Fern commented to no one in particular.

"I'll help," said one of the roustabouts.

Ten minutes later there was a nice fire burning, sheltered from the wind by some low brush. Everyone had pitched in gathering wood, and there was a considerable pile of branches and sticks nearby. Danny scouted the little island and found nothing of concern.

"Two of you men get over here and lay down," Fern said. "Make a pocket for me and the young'un twixt ya. I gotta keep this baby warm tonight."

Shortly, all the men were sprawled around the fire, two of them cradling Fern and her baby. Isaac was snuggled against the sergeant's back.

Chapter Eighteen

The *Barnard Clinton* eased up to what passed for a wharf at Omaha. Omaha had not even existed twelve years before this day. A group of speculators had laid out the town, counting on the routing of the transcontinental railroad, and they had hit the jackpot. The niceties of a wharf were a low priority in the rush to profit from the huge undertaking of laying rails across Nebraska.

The arrival of a steamboat was eagerly anticipated, as the supply of goods could not keep pace with the population growth. Before the stages were down, wagons were being maneuvered into position to take the freight consigned to Omaha to its next destination, whether it be local retailers or companies that would continue its transport to the frontier.

Everyone on the *Clinton* had a job or an objective. As soon as the vessel was tied up properly, the roustabouts, with direction by both mates, began gathering freight that was due to be off-loaded, moving upriver freight to one side so that wagons could be brought into the cargo bay.

The engineers began preparing the mud drums for cleaning. As soon as the boilers cooled, there would be no more power on the vessel, so preparations had to be made to take that into account. The remaining steam was being used to power the doctor engine and water pump to extinguish the fires in the fireboxes; that, of course, began reducing the steam until the doctor engine would no longer run. Then the safety valves were lifted on all the boilers to eliminate the last vestige of pressure. Drains were opened on the mud drums, and the boilers, being higher, drained their water into the mud drums and then into the Missouri River. The next task was to wait, wait for the boilers and the mud drum to cool enough for the maintenance crew to remove the end caps on the mud drums and wash out the accumulation of sludge, sand, and debris. While this was going on, there was other maintenance to perform on the valve linkages, the valves themselves, the pitman arms, the steering cables and pulleys, and the paddle wheel.

Weedeater had recruited another roustabout to assist him in protecting the boat, the passengers, and the cargo. Jimbo was as tall and lean as Weedeater was thick and short. He was tough, hard, and unafraid of bad odds. He had been a brawler until enlisting in the Army at the outbreak of the war. A hard, no-nonsense commanding officer had harnessed his energy and kept him out of trouble. Now he was ready for action as a kind of deputy to Weedeater. He was not proficient with guns, so Weedeater had given him his shotgun instead of a rifle, and Weedeater carried the repeater. Weedeater had taken up a position in front of the pilothouse, and Jimbo was patrolling the bow and the stages as the wagons came and went.

The captain stepped onto the deck in front of the pilothouse and joined Weedeater. "Mr. Koslosky, if you can be spared, I have a job for you."

"Yes, sir. I don't see any problems down there."

"Very well. Find the purser before he goes to town and accompany him to my cabin. Don't take any excuses. This isn't a request." The captain turned without waiting for a reply and walked to his cabin.

Weedeater signaled to Jimbo that he would be away from his post and then descended the main stairs to the boiler deck. He entered the main salon and headed for the purser's office.

Jack Galloway was gathering his paperwork and requisitions

for a trip to town to restock the *Clinton*. He looked up as Weedeater came to the door of his office. He didn't have a high opinion of Weedeater; he thought the man was too sure of himself with no good reason. His clothes didn't look clean, his face was never clean-shaven, and Galloway was sure that Weedeater couldn't read or write. He was, in Galloway's opinion, a person with little ability to better himself in the modern world. He had his papers under his arm and started to walk past Weedeater without acknowledging him.

"The captain wants to speak to you in his cabin, Mr. Galloway," Weedeater said.

"I'll see him as soon as I return from town," Galloway said.

Weedeater blocked his path. "Now."

"Get out of my way." Galloway shifted his papers to his left hand and put his right hand on the butt of his hideaway gun.

Weedeater was not intimidated. "You can walk, or I can carry you."

Galloway suspected that if he went to the captain's cabin, there would be no good news. On the other hand, if he defied this roustabout and went to town, it might cost him his job and therefore his bonus for accomplishing his evil plan. He sized up the little roustabout and decided his best interest lay in going to the captain's cabin. There was nothing he had to do in Omaha that couldn't wait.

"You little river scum, go make someone else sick at their stomach. I'll see the captain."

Weedeater, ignoring the insult and remembering the captain's explicit instructions, said, "I'll go with you." Galloway snorted and brushed past Weedeater, who followed him out of the main salon and up the stairs to the Texas deck. When they reached the captain's cabin, Weedeater knocked on the closed door. The captain opened it.

"Come in, Mr. Galloway. You too, Mr. Koslosky." Both men entered, and the captain returned to his seat behind his desk.

Galloway stood, waiting for the captain to speak. A full minute passed as the captain looked over the papers spread in front of him. Galloway became more and more restless and finally began to speak.

"Captain, I . . ."

The captain held his hand up for silence. He looked up at Galloway, and the look caused Galloway to feel a chill all over.

"Empty your pockets on the desk, Mr. Galloway."

"What do you mean?" Galloway asked angrily.

"Now!" the captain said firmly.

Galloway looked around as if there might be someone around to help him out of this situation. Weedeater made ready to use his rifle. Galloway had no choice but to comply. He emptied his pockets. There was a folding knife, a watch, three gold coins, and three keys. The captain put the keys in the drawer of his desk.

"Take off your hat, coat, and tie, and lay them on my bed."

Galloway was trembling with rage, but he did as the captain ordered.

"Give me your pistol." As the captain said this, Weedeater levered a cartridge into his rifle and brought the barrel up. Galloway slowly removed the pistol from its holster and dropped it carelessly on the captain's desk. The captain gave him a black look, and then he picked up the pistol and removed the caps.

"Your accounts are short by almost four hundred dollars. Mr. Koslosky will escort you off the *Clinton*. Your service is terminated. I'll go through your office and, if the missing money is found, I'll pack up your belongings and send them to the marshal in Omaha. If not, I'll assume you have sent the four hundred dollars off the boat, and we'll keep your belongings against what you have stolen."

"You can't do this!" Galloway shouted.

The captain responded calmly. "Yes, I can. I thought about

putting you off the boat fifty miles below Nebraska City. This is kinder than you deserve." The captain addressed Weedeater next. "Mr. Koslosky, take this man to the wharf. If he tries to reboard the *Clinton* at any time, shoot him."

"Let's go, Galloway!" Weedeater said, and he stood aside to let Galloway exit the cabin. Then he followed him, just as the captain had ordered, all the way to the wharf where he watched Galloway stalk up the banks to Omaha, without money, without credentials, without prospects.

Just before sunrise that morning, Danny awoke under a cloudy sky. This was good, he thought. The men would not get overheated as the group tried to overtake the *Clinton.* The fire was burning brightly; someone had built it back up. He looked around and noticed that the boy, Isaac, was missing.

The island was only a short distance from the western shore. Danny walked to the shallow channel that defined the island and he spotted Isaac, five hundred yards upstream, standing on the western bank. As Danny watched, the boy yanked at something in the water. Danny didn't have time to speculate on what the boy might be doing. In a matter of seconds Isaac dragged a fish out of the water and kicked it hard into the bushes. Then he went to the fish and removed something from its mouth and began feeling through the grass on the bank, for what, Danny didn't know. The next sound was the baby fussing back at the fire. Danny turned around to see Fern slowly standing up and stepping over the men who had provided her with warmth during the night, babe in arms. He walked over to join her, satisfied that Isaac was in no danger.

"It looks like Isaac is catching breakfast for us," he said as he approached.

"I 'spect so," Fern answered. "You'll have to 'scuse us. I'm gonna give the young 'un his breakfast."

"Of course," Danny replied and turned away to watch Isaac again as Fern walked a short distance away, singing softly to her baby.

Isaac caught two more fish and then began wading back to the island, that being easier than struggling through the bushes on the bank. Fern met Isaac as he forded the channel between the island and the bank.

"Give me them fish and your knife, Isaac, and hold this young 'un while I make breakfast."

None of the roustabouts and soldiers, having stayed up all night the night before, was anxious to get up from their warm spots on the sand. The smell of fish roasting over the fire brought them awake, however, and soon they were all tearing off pieces of fish from where Fern had laid them, steaming, on a flat rock.

Danny sat next to Isaac, who was also enjoying the fruits of his efforts. "How did you catch those fish, Isaac?" He wanted to see if he could get the boy to speak.

Isaac pulled a coil of string from the pocket of his overalls. One end was tied around a grove in the middle of a stick about two inches long, sharpened on both ends. He showed it to Danny but said nothing.

Fern, observing the one-sided conversation, offered the explanation. "He spears a 'hopper on the stick and drops it where he knows a fish is waitin'," she said. "Then when he feels the fish swallow the 'hopper, he yanks on the string and the stick wedges sideways in the fish's throat."

Danny looked at Isaac. "That's a good trick, Isaac." Isaac was silent.

"His daddy taught him," Fern said. "His daddy was real smart about things like that." She rocked her baby as she spoke. "He was good to us." She said it matter-of-factly, as if Isaac's father had not met a horrible death in their presence just two days ago.

"Good job, Isaac. We all needed to eat," Danny praised. Isaac put the coil of string and wooden spear back into his pocket.

Danny stood up and looked around the little island. "Let's pull one of the yawls into the brush and hide it. We'll make better time, and the *Clinton* can pick it up on her way downstream." No one disagreed, and they quickly accomplished the task.

Danny helped Fern and her baby into the other yawl where it sat on the sand. Then the men lined up on either side and slid it across the sand into the river. In minutes they were pulling against the current with renewed energy. They were almost twenty-five miles downriver from Omaha.

Chapter Nineteen

Robert Pruitt entered the pilothouse exactly on time at fifteen minutes before four in the afternoon. David Erickson, his mate, followed him in. Charles Felden and Steve Allenby were there to give their reports and turn the vessel over to the B-watch. Captain Culpepper was not there, which was unusual, but the exchange of information proceeded without him.

"The ends are off two of the mud drums. The men inside have removed about half of the sludge. It's brutal." Allenby was referring to the fact that the drums retained so much heat. But it wasn't possible to wait until they cooled completely, and in any case, the work in the narrow, unventilated space would be difficult, no matter what the temperature. Allenby continued. "Brown is rotating men so no one has to stay inside too long."

"Good idea," Erickson said. "I'll see that Van Dusen does the same." Everyone present knew that Peter Van Dusen would be less sympathetic to his workers, and they nodded to indicate their approval.

Allenby had more. "The next time, let's isolate the starboard boilers, bring down the larboard side, and use the pump to help cool the drums. We can pull the caps earlier that way."

Erickson nodded his head. "And then, while we reassemble the larboard side, we can start working on the starboard. By the time we get those caps off, we might have enough steam in the larboard boilers to put the pump on line."

"That's what I was thinking," Allenby said. "I'll write it up and give it to the captain." Allenby picked up a stack of papers and handed them to Erickson. "I've marked off the freight that has been unloaded. We're done with the railroad equipment; there's just some small consignments to people in Omaha, and that won't take more than an hour. The freight to come on-board is all at the wharf and doesn't amount to much."

"If it weren't for the mud drums, we could be on our way before sunset," Pruitt remarked.

Felden commented drily, "That and recovering our men and the two yawls."

"Yes, of course, I meant that too," Pruitt hastened to say. He was embarrassed that he had not mentioned the lost crew and boats in his observation.

"With a lot of the freight out of the hold, I've got two men down there, caulking. She's been making a little water since St. Joseph. You'll want to finish that before you start loading," Allenby said.

"All right. After the freight is loaded, we'll put those men on repacking the pump seals," Erickson said.

"The captain is in town buying supplies," Allenby said. "He should be back soon, and there'll be more goods to bring on-board. He might also be trying to hire another purser."

Captain Culpepper was on the wharf, directing a wagonload of supplies onto the stage to be unloaded. He had not been successful in recruiting a new purser, so he had taken on the duties himself. As the teamster drove the wagon across the stage, a man with a badge rode up on a horse.

"Captain Culpepper?" he asked.

The captain turned to face the man. "Yes," he said.

"I want to talk to you about Jack Galloway."

"Very well."

The man dismounted and tied his horse to a post. "Galloway claims you have stolen his personal belongings, and that you owe him passage back to St. Louis."

"He's a liar and a thief."

"I need to see his quarters to see if a law has been broken."

"I'm the law on the *Clinton*," the captain stated firmly.

The marshal started to say something and then held up his hands, palms forward. "Whoa. Let's start over," he said in a conciliatory tone. "I'm Rake Angleton, the marshal in Omaha. Jack Galloway came to my office with a complaint. I have no choice but to investigate."

"Galloway stole four hundred dollars from the *Clinton*. If it is returned, his belongings will be returned. I haven't had the opportunity to search his quarters. The missing money may or may not be there. But I can show you his bookkeeping to prove what I say is true."

Rake Angleton could size up a person quickly. He made a correct assessment of the captain's character. He had previously assessed Galloway's character and had not liked the result. "All right, Captain. I don't need to see your books. If you would take care of searching his quarters soon, I'll proceed based on what you find or don't."

"Fair enough. I'll send word to you within the hour."

"I'll wait here," Angleton said.

Harvey Blake had headed into Omaha as soon as the *Clinton* tied up at the wharf. He wanted to procure various materials that would help him accomplish his objective of putting the *Clinton* permanently out of service. He had several ideas and therefore had to visit a variety of retailers to find all that he needed. He had come onboard with ten pounds of black powder, knowing that buying it along the way might be difficult and might arouse suspicions. What he was looking for now were some specific hardware items that would not arouse any suspicions. As he stepped out of a store he saw Jack Galloway, hatless and coatless, walking angrily up the boardwalk toward him. He waited, wondering what Galloway was up to. Galloway saw him and stopped in front of him.

"We've got trouble!" Galloway said.

"What?"

"I've been fired."

Blake said nothing, waiting for more explanation.

"Didn't you hear?" he repeated. "I've been fired."

"All right. Now what?" Blake was not happy. He couldn't proceed without Galloway's help. Although he was fairly confident that he could disable the *Clinton*, he didn't know who had hired Galloway and what he would have to do to get paid.

Galloway related the story of his firing, omitting the fact that he had been fired for skimming, blaming it instead on the captain's intolerance of nonmilitary methods of performing his duties. As far as adapting the plan to his new circumstances, he had nothing to offer, no ideas. But Blake did.

"How far upriver will the boat be by daylight tomorrow morning?" Blake asked.

"Somewhere between five and ten miles. Depending on when they cast off."

"All right. Get yourself upstream somewhere where the steamer will have to come close to the bank. Start a fire. I won't do anything until the boat passes the fire. Then I'll fix it so it drifts back down past you. Be ready."

"What're you gonna do?"

"Plenty. When I get done they won't have power or steerage. And there'll be enough going on that the crew won't be in a position to interfere when I kill the captain and rob the safe."

"You're gonna do that by yourself?" Galloway asked.

"No. I know a couple of guys in Omaha who'll come aboard tonight."

Galloway felt threatened. His only leverage was that he knew where the payday was coming from. And that might not be enough, especially if Blake was going to be satisfied with merely robbing the *Clinton*'s safe. He had to come up with something. "All right. I have an idea that will fit right in."

Blake would have preferred it if Galloway had had no ideas, but he had to listen. "Yeah?" he queried.

"I met an Indian on the waterfront. I thought I was gonna need a little help to get back on the *Clinton*. I told him I might be able to give him some work."

"Bad idea. We've got all the help we need." Blake's eyes narrowed as he said this. He didn't think Galloway was bright enough to accomplish anything as complicated as this was going to be, nor did he think the fired purser was able to take care of himself if teamed up with someone who might or might not be willing to share the spoils.

For his part, Galloway was suspicious of Blake. Galloway would be outnumbered and on the shore. But he realized he didn't have to face Blake down now. The Indian he had met looked capable and ruthless and would help even the odds. He gave in. "You're probably right. That's that, then. I'll see you in the morning."

The two men didn't shake hands when they parted.

Captain Culpepper walked up the stage to the waiting marshal. He was carrying a leather bag.

"Marshal," the captain said, "I found the missing money in the purser's office. I packed up his possessions in his bag. You can return it to him or I'll leave it with the wharfmaster."

"I'll take it, Captain," Angleton said as he mounted and took the bag from the captain. "Let's hope this finishes it."

"He's been warned that I'll kill him if he comes onboard the *Clinton*."

Angleton would have liked to express his disapproval of that statement, but both men were distracted by the sound of a steam whistle on a sidewheeler that had made its approach while they were talking. On a three-hundred-foot tow behind the sidewheeler *Platte Valley* was the yawl belonging to the *Clinton*. In the yawl the captain was pleased to see all his missing crew, and surprised to also see a young woman and a boy. As he watched, the *Platte Valley* cast the yawl adrift, and the men took up their oars and began rowing toward the wharf while the sidewheeler maneuvered to the berth signaled by the wharfmaster.

"This is welcome news, Marshal. You'll excuse me, please."

"Good luck on your voyage, Captain." He slapped the reins on his horse's neck and rode back toward town.

Chapter Twenty

Danny guided the yawl alongside the *Clinton* and the men shipped their oars. Two roustabouts grabbed the lines and made the yawl fast to the steamer. Danny took the baby from Fern so she could climb over the gunwales and board the steamer, and then he handed the child to her.

A roustabout leaned over the edge of the hurricane deck and shouted down to the yawl crew. "Puttin' 'er away?" Danny signaled yes, and the hoist lines came down. Danny walked Fern to the main cabin, followed by Isaac.

In the main salon, Danny found Weedeater. "Weedeater, this young woman and her boy are hungry. Take them to the kitchen and see they get fed." Then he added, "Her name is Fern, and the boy's name is Isaac."

"Sure, Danny." Weedeater looked the frail young woman over and decided she was probably a lot tougher than she looked, but not unattractive to the rough riverman.

The yawl crew, four roustabouts and two soldiers, had followed Danny in. He turned around and addressed them. "You men follow Weedeater into the kitchen. There's no sense in waiting until supper." They had had only three fish among them since leaving the shabby cabin two days ago.

"I have to see the captain, Weed, and then I'll be back down to get some grub for myself and tell you all about it. Take good care of Fern and Isaac. And the baby."

Weedeater took Fern's arm; she started to pull away, but

something in his manner reassured her, and she walked beside him, feeling safer than she had for a long time. Isaac followed as he led the procession into the kitchen. Danny left the main salon and climbed to the Texas deck. The captain, having seen him bring the yawl in, was waiting eagerly at the top of the stairs.

"Mr. Barton, it's good to have you back. I'll take your report in the pilothouse." He turned and walked forward on the Texas deck.

A-watch was on duty, so Felden was in the pilothouse doing chart work. He looked up as Danny walked in, then stood up, nodding his head with a trace of a smile. "Welcome back, Danny," he said.

"Thanks, Charles." Danny put his hands on his hips. "Captain, we caught up to the outlaws after dark two days ago. We killed all of them in a gunfight. The other yawl was slowing us down too much. I left it in the bushes on an island just this side of the Platte River mouth."

"The woman?" the captain asked.

"Fern. Don't know her last name. She and a man named Carl White had moved into a tumbledown cabin on the bank. Her husband died a bit ago. The outlaws killed Carl White. Neither of them had anything of value. The boy, Isaac, is White's son. The baby is Fern's."

"None of you were hurt in the shootout?"

"No, sir."

"Are the woman and the children healthy?"

"Yes, and tough as leather."

"Very well. We can use Fern in the kitchen or put her off here at Omaha if she prefers."

"My guess is that she'll stay with the boat. They're all getting fed right now."

"The men too?"

"Yes, sir."

"Good. Good job, Mr. Barton." He patted Danny on the shoulder. "You should know that I dismissed the purser with prejudice. He is not to be allowed to board the *Clinton* under any circumstances. I was unable to hire a replacement in Omaha. The bartender, Skeet, will handle the dining room, and I'll promote one of the kitchen staff to supervise the kitchen and maid work."

Danny nodded and the captain continued.

"Weedeater has Jimbo helping him keep peace. Weedeater was wounded in the fight in the main salon. Keep Jimbo until you're sure Weedeater is adequately recovered."

"All right, sir," Danny said, and the captain went on.

"The work on the mud drums has gone well. We'll be ready to cast off in the morning. We'll bypass Council Bluffs this time and make all progress possible to Fort Benton." The captain took a moment to think something over and then spoke. "The sun will be down soon, Mr. Barton. If you can wait to eat until then, let's take supper together."

"I would enjoy that, sir. I'll get cleaned up and meet you at sundown in the main cabin."

"Very well, Mr. Barton."

Danny left and went to his cabin, leaving only the captain and Felden in the pilothouse.

"Captain," Felden said, "that's a pretty good man there."

"I agree, Mr. Felden. But I am reminded of something else. You and I were going to sit down together."

"Yes, sir."

"As soon as we get the *Clinton* lined out above Omaha, we'll take care of that."

"Yes, sir."

There was a tap on the pilothouse door, which was standing open. It was Abigail.

"Captain Culpepper?"

The captain turned at the sound of her voice. "Abigail. Come in."

Abigail stepped into the pilothouse. "I thought perhaps we could eat together this evening," she said.

The captain considered for a moment. He didn't want to back out of his supper with Barton. "I have already asked Mr. Barton to dine with me. If you don't mind having Mr. Barton join us, I'm sure he will have some interesting stories to tell." He was disappointed that he had made a commitment to Danny and fully expected her to turn him down.

"How interesting. I'm looking forward to it. I'll see you soon, then." She touched his sleeve and then left the pilothouse. The captain also left a few minutes later and descended to the main cabin to talk to Skeet.

"Mr. Skecher, is everything in order?" The captain wanted to know if the bartender was learning the duties of the purser.

"I think so, Captain. Here is the new passenger roster. The Willises have checked out of the Vermont cabin. We have four Army Officers, twenty-six enlisted men, fifteen male civilians, six women, and seventeen children. Seventeen roustabouts, including the two firemen and two strikers, nine kitchen staff, and four maids. Counting the officers, there are one hundred seven people. Cabin assignments are the same except for the Vermont cabin, which is unoccupied. The main changes are five extra men booked into the main cabin, and the family that Danny, uh, Mr. Barton brought back."

"Very well, Mr. Skecher, has anyone asked for the Vermont cabin?"

"No, sir."

"Let me know before you assign anyone to it. Did Major Williams get taken to the undertaker?"

"Yes, sir. Here's the ledger and the money from the additional passengers. The foundlings have not paid anything, of course."

"No. They may not wish to voyage with us. I'll find that out soon. By the way, you will begin receiving Mr. Galloway's salary immediately."

"Thank you, Captain. Oh . . ." Skeet said as the captain started to walk away.

"Yes?"

"There is also the baby. There are one hundred and eight people onboard."

"Yes, of course. Thank you, Mr. Skecher."

The captain walked into the kitchen. He paused at the open door. Preparations were being made to feed the first-class passengers, and the room, warm and humid, was full of motion and noise. His eyes settled on Fern, who was working in front of one of the ovens, wearing a clean white apron over her tattered dress. Nearby, Isaac was holding the baby. The captain watched the small young woman for a few minutes, marveling at her strength and dexterity in handling large pots and pans full of food. The maid, Eleanor, was working not far from where the captain stood and he motioned to her. She took a minute to turn her job over to another worker and came to him.

"How much time did Mr. Galloway spend in the kitchen, Eleanor?" he inquired.

"Shoot, Cap'n, we never saw him."

"Who decides what to serve and how to prepare it?"

"We all does," she said, putting her hands on her hips. "We know what we're doin'."

"Who knows the most?"

"I reckon I do, but I ain't sure we'd all agree." She chuckled.

The captain didn't smile. "I'll take your word. I intend to post a notice that you are in charge. You'll be receiving fifty cents more per week."

Eleanor's face lit up. "Whew, Cap'n, I ain't never bossed no one before."

"Your first job will be to find out if the waif"—the captain nodded toward Fern—"wants to stay onboard and work. If so, she is to receive the salary that you formerly did."

"Yes, sir."

"Let me know if she intends to work. If she doesn't, she'll have to leave the boat before we cast off in the morning."

"Yes, sir."

The captain left the kitchen. First call for supper was only minutes away; he had just enough time to change his shirt and tie before sitting down with Abigail. And Danny Barton.

Chapter Twenty-one

Harvey Blake leaned across the table to say something to the two men; he didn't want anyone else in the saloon to hear what he had to say.

"Get down there before midnight. The bartender will take your money and assign you a berth. He turns in at midnight, so don't waste time. You each have a job. You know what it is," Blake said in a low voice. "When you get onboard, look the boat over and find the places I told you about. Then we'll get together and make sure there'll be no mistakes. I want to get this done before we get to Sioux City."

"Hunnerd dollars each?" one of the men asked.

"That's right," Blake answered.

"Half now."

"No. Full pay after . . ." He didn't finish. "But here's your fare." Blake quickly passed the cash across the table. "Nothing else until tomorrow."

"Whadda you get?"

"More," was all Blake would say.

"How much more?"

Blake didn't answer, and his look told his questioner that he was on dangerous ground.

"I guess that's fair enough," the man said. "But if we find out you're makin' a killin' with our help, we'll come back for our share."

"What I get is of no concern to you. You're going to make three months' wages in one or two days. Take it or leave it."

"We'll take it. Let's get out of here, Dink," the man said to the other.

Blake wanted to be back onboard before his two hirelings, so he also left the bar and walked quickly to the waterfront.

Chapter Twenty-two

Why do you suppose the outlaws stopped at the cabin instead of continuing down the river?" Abigail asked Danny. The three had finished their meal and were engrossed in conversation.

"I guess they didn't believe they would be followed. After killing a man." Danny glanced at the captain. If they had known the captain as well as he did, they would have realized that they would not be safe anywhere near the river.

"Why did they kill Mr. White?"

"It was senseless," Danny said, shrugging.

"How old is this young woman, Mr. Barton?" Abigail asked.

"I don't know," Danny replied, "except for her eyes, she looks like a schoolgirl." He and Abigail had dominated the conversation at the supper table. Danny was a little uncomfortable in the presence of both the captain and the attractive Miss DeMille but was forthcoming and matter-of-fact in telling the story of the chase and confrontation to the beautiful woman. The captain seemed quite content, perhaps even pleased, to be a listener only.

"Where did she come from?" Abigail asked.

"She and her husband spent the winter on the Platte River. He died before spring, shortly after she gave birth to the baby boy. When the ice went out, she began trying to make her way down the Platte River. After a week of difficult travel with little food, she met an Indian couple who fed her and sheltered her for a few days before leaving her to make their own way west. She actually made it to the Missouri, where she met Carl White and his son, Isaac. Together, they found the abandoned cabin and were resting there when the outlaws walked in. They killed Carl White immediately, and a few minutes later, we showed up. If we had been a half hour earlier, we might have saved his life."

"How terrible!" Abigail exclaimed.

"The sum total of her possessions is the dress she was wearing and a small blanket," Danny said. "We had time to gather up anything else before we left the cabin, and there wasn't anything."

"What will become of her and her baby?" Abigail asked. She directed this question to the captain, knowing that he had more ability to influence her future than Danny, or anyone else.

"I have offered her a position on the *Clinton*," the captain said. "Beyond that, I can't say."

"Her future does not seem very bright," Abigail said. It was not meant as a criticism of the captain. It was a comment on the situation that had fallen in front of them. Nor was Captain Culpepper offended; he nodded agreement.

Danny said, "It's certainly brighter than it was. There are many widows in America now. Some of them are in worse circumstances than Fern."

"I am concerned that the widows of whom you speak, the freed slaves, both men and women, and the crippled veterans will be forgotten in the rush to take advantage of the opportunities that peace affords. The nation has squandered much of its wealth on war. It is time, fairly or unfairly, to rebuild that wealth." This was a lengthy statement for the captain to make, and it surprised both Abigail and Danny.

"Can that be done and still see to the needs of the less fortunate?" Abigail asked.

"The man who could have brought that about has been killed," Culpepper said, referring to Abraham Lincoln.

Eleanor came to the table, carrying a tray of cakes for dessert. "Cap'n, we wanted you to have sump'n special." She placed the tray on the table.

"That's a nice surprise, Eleanor. Is there enough for the other first-class passengers?"

"Yes, sir. Fern be bringin' more for them now."

"And will she, Fern, be staying with us?"

"Yes, sir. She got nowhere else to go. She say the boy stayin' too."

"Very well. Does she have sleeping accommodations?"

"She do, in the ladies' cabin, but the boy can't be sleepin' there."

"No, of course not. Is Isaac still in the kitchen?"

"No, sir, the baby be fussin', and he walkin' him out yonder." She gestured toward the walkway just outside the main cabin. "Too hot for any baby in the kitchen."

"Very well. Thank you, Eleanor." Eleanor returned to the kitchen, and Captain Culpepper rose from his chair. "Miss Demille, Mr. Barton, excuse me for a moment. I'll return shortly. Please enjoy the cakes." He strode to the exit and out onto the walkway where he found Isaac.

"Young man, do you know who I am?" the captain asked. Isaac shifted the baby to his left arm but did not speak. Captain Culpepper sat down on a bench, which put his face nearly level with Isaac's. "This is my boat. I'm the captain," he said, searching the boy's eyes for a sign of understanding.

The boy's eyes followed his every move but showed no emotion.

"Did you get enough to eat?"

This time Culpepper thought he saw a quick smile but it vanished just as quickly, leaving the boy's face blank once again. Still the boy didn't answer.

"We have to decide where you are to sleep at night." At this statement, the boy's face took on several expressions, and the captain thought he was making progress. "I'll get you a blanket, and find you a place in the cargo bay."

The boy finally spoke. "I have to stay with the woman that my father and I found."

The captain tried to evaluate the boy's statement—not just the words but the tone of his voice, his inflection. "And why is that, Isaac?"

"I take care of the baby some."

The captain could accept this logic. If Fern had to take care of her baby, she wouldn't be much help on the *Clinton*. "Very well, Isaac. I'll find you both a place." The captain patted Isaac on the head and went back into the kitchen to speak with Eleanor.

"Eleanor, the Vermont cabin is unoccupied at the moment. Tell Fern and Isaac they can stay in that cabin for now. Find a box they can use for a crib."

"Yes, sir."

The captain left the kitchen and rejoined Abigail in the dining room. By now the main cabin passengers were finishing their meals, and the roustabouts were coming in. Danny was not at the table.

"Mr. Barton excused himself, Captain. He could scarcely keep his eyes open."

"Yes, he's had a busy two days."

"He seems to be a very bright young man," Abigail said.

"Yes." The captain remembered Danny in one of the final battles of the Civil War. Culpepper, a colonel at that time, was facing a desperate counterattack by a numerically inferior force of Confederates when his horse was shot from under him. Wounded, Danny gave his mount to Culpepper and held his ground, armed only with a pistol. As Culpepper was trying to rally his less-than-motivated officers, their position was overrun and Danny was captured. Culpepper knew that Danny was more than bright; he was a warrior with a tremendous sense of duty and little fear. That was why Culpepper had found him after the war and hired him to be the "sheriff" on the *Barnard Clinton*. He decided not to share his attachment to Danny with Abigail. For her part, she suspected there was more to Danny and the captain than she knew.

"He's more than just an employee to you, isn't he?" she asked.

"Yes. I have found I can rely on him with little reservation."

"He's like a son, isn't he?"

The captain didn't want to answer this question. He didn't think his own son was made of the same material of which Danny Barton was, and it caused him sorrow. They were the same age, and Robert Pruitt had had more advantages than Danny had, but he had not matured in the same way.

"Miss Demille, allow me to walk you to your cabin, and then I must attend to my duties."

Abigail would not let the evening end this way. "Captain, I think it's time for us to share more than light conversation. I want you to know something about me. And I hope from this moment that I may learn more about you without concern of offending."

The captain was taken aback and at a temporary loss for words, but before he could respond, the second mate, David Erickson, came to the table.

"Captain?"

"Yes, Mr. Erickson."

"We started filling the boilers."

"That's fine, Mr. Erickson. Thank you."

"We hope to have the larboard boilers filled by midnight. We'll build the fires when they're nearly full and then use the doctor engine to pump the starboard boilers full. We should have full steam up by four A.M."

"Turn out all the roustabouts so that no one has to spend

more than fifteen minutes on the pump handle. Use two men at a time on the pump handles, then rest them for a half hour between times. There will be a wagon at ten P.M. with two kegs of cold beer. Ration the beer at one-half glass for each fifteen minutes of pumping."

"Yes, sir!" The mate knew this would be welcome news to the roustabouts. "There's one other thing, sir."

"Yes?"

"Van Dusen said the variable cutoff valve needs a new bushing. He didn't discover this until he began reassembling it. There aren't any bushings in Omaha; they may be available in Council Bluffs. He says it's got a few more miles in it, but after that he doesn't know."

"What do you think, Mr. Erickson?"

"These are the new style, Captain. They're said to be twice as durable as the old ones, but I really couldn't say for sure."

"Very well, I'll see Mr. Van Dusen. A stop at Council Bluffs would entail an unacceptable delay. Is that all?"

"Yes, sir." Erickson left the main cabin to supervise the pumping.

"Abigail, you'll have to excuse me. Once again, I need to attend to business."

Abigail was still not going to be dismissed as easy as that. She stood up when the captain did and came to his side. Standing on her toes, she kissed him quickly on the cheek in full view of the entire main cabin. Then she walked away, leaving the captain stunned.

For just a moment the captain had the impulse to go after Abigail, but his sense of duty compelled him to the stairs where he descended to the cargo bay and the engine room to find out more about the bushing.

Peter Van Dusen was known for being cantankerous, but his belligerence was usually muted when in the presence of authority. That was not the case this evening. He had been on duty almost continuously since the *Clinton* tied up at Omaha, working with William Brown to do the maintenance that couldn't be done when underway. Brown had just left for his cabin, hoping to get one or two hours of sleep before going on his regular watch at midnight.

"I can't guarantee five miles of operation with the cutoff valve linkage in this condition," Van Dusen said, testily.

Engineers, by some reckoning, were the most important officers on the riverboats, but the lowest paid, least acknowledged, and first blamed when something went wrong. Manufacturers of steam engines were mostly to blame for this phenomenon. They commonly boasted that their engines could be operated by anyone after only a few weeks training, when, in fact, the engines required considerable knowledge of science and a high degree of mechanical skill. Many river disasters were caused by inadequate knowledge of steam and inept operation of the tremendous power of the engines.

"Show me," the captain said.

"Here's the old bushing," Van Dusen said, pointing to a large brass ring on his workbench. "It's supposed to be the same thickness all the way around."

"Show me where it is in the linkage."

Van Dusen stepped over to the valve linkage, partially disassembled, and pointed to the place where the bushing was supposed to be.

"What happens if you don't replace it?"

"I can't control the speed of the engines."

The captain doubted this statement. "Not at all?" he asked.

"Not as precisely as that wet-behind-the-ears pilot wants, that's a certainty." Van Dusen was referring to Robert Pruitt, who had still not won the respect of his engineer. He was ignorant of the fact that Pruitt was Culpepper's son. "I'll have to adjust it and grease it every few hours, and in the end, it will fail, and the linkage will fall apart."

"And then what happens?"

"We'll have to run on one engine and only use the other at full speed or dead stop."

"All right. If that's what happens, you'll have to deal with it. We're not going to stop at Council Bluffs or Sioux City. There may be parts at Fort Pierre."

"I won't be responsible for the way this engine operates!" Van Dusen said firmly.

Perhaps it was the memory of Abigail's quick kiss that mellowed the captain, or perhaps he was as tired as the others. He had slept little, not just since arriving at Omaha, but in truth, since Danny Barton and his crew had left the steamer to pursue the outlaws in the yawl. Ordinarily, he would have let Van Dusen know that proper operation of the engines in *all* events was a condition of employment on the *Clinton*. This time he only said, "Mr. Dusen, I have full confidence that you can deal with this inconvenience without jeopardizing the engines, the vessel, or the passengers. Pass on this discussion to William Brown at change of watch. Good evening." And he turned and strode away.

Chapter Twenty-three

The boilers on the *Barnard Clinton* were fairly modern but quite crude by locomotive standards, as were all steamboat boilers. There were two larboard boilers and two starboard boilers. Each pair of boilers sat side by side on a firebox. There were no sight glasses; the fireman was required to periodically open trycocks, or small valves on the side of each boiler. The lower trycock must emit hot water; the upper trycock should emit steam. And even if the fireman found that to be the case, there was still no indication of the exact water level inside the boiler.

Each boiler was also equipped with a pressure gauge of poor quality, compared to one found on a locomotive, and a safety valve. The safety valve was held in closed position by gravity working on a long lever on which a sliding weight was attached. The opening pressure of the safety valve was adjusted by sliding the weight, or "pea," closer or farther from the pivot of the lever, the fulcrum.

In spite of the inexactitude of this system, the A-watch fireman, by keeping track of the efforts on the manual pump, and from experience, knew within an inch where the water was. He also knew how fast he could bring the fires up in the fireboxes. As soon as the bottom of the boiler was covered with water, the small fires in the firebox began heating it. If the boiler was heated unevenly, or if fire impinged on the plates without water being on the other side, the plates would warp and begin leaking. Once this started, it was impossible to stop and usually meant that the boiler would have to be rebuilt. It became a race between the men on the pump and the stokers at the firebox, with the fireman as referee maintaining an equilibrium so that when the water level was finally above the lower trycocks, the firebox was glowing red from end to end and both boilers were producing steam. And it came out exactly so.

The next challenge was to keep the larboard boilers level between the trycocks, while the doctor pump, now supplied with steam, began to fill the starboard boilers. And the fireman was up to that challenge also. Before four A.M., the *Clinton*'s boilers were producing over one hundred pounds of steam and the fireman reported this to the mate who would inform the captain at the change of watch in the pilothouse. This entire procedure was known on the *Clinton* as the "upriver" method of bringing a cold steamboat into operation. It was simpler in a boatyard or at a wharf catering to maintenance.

"By the time we get untied, we'll have a hundred twenty pounds of steam, Captain," Allenby, the first mate, said. "It's coming up fast."

"Very well, Mr. Allenby." The captain knew that his entire crew had worked without rest to make the layover at Omaha as brief as possible. Although it was still ten minutes before the hour, the captain wanted his crew, especially the officers, to get as much rest as possible. "If there's nothing else, you are dismissed this moment."

"No, nothing else," Allenby said. "Thank you, Captain." But without making a show of it, he lingered in the pilothouse, not entirely comfortable with the captain's abbreviating his watch.

"Mr. Pruitt," the captain said, "release Mr. Felden and take over now."

"Yes, sir." Pruitt stepped up to the wheel.

"Mr. Erickson, get under way without delay," the captain told the B-watch mate.

"Yes, sir." David Erickson left the pilothouse to organize the deck crew for casting off from the Omaha wharf. Steve Allenby and Charles Felden left for their cabins.

The captain looked around. There was only the pilot, himself, and Danny Barton in the pilothouse.

"Mr. Barton, did you get enough rest?" Danny had been asleep since leaving the captain's table the previous evening.

"Yes, sir," Barton said. "I sent Weedeater and Jimbo to get some rest. There are quite a few passengers still up at this time, wanting to be awake for the departure. I'm going down to the main cabin now to make sure they all get bedded down without problems. They'll want the bar opened, but Skeet needs some sleep too."

"Very good. Let's see if we can keep everyone quiet until noon."

"Yes, sir." Barton turned to leave the pilothouse.

"I'll be in my cabin," the captain said.

The departure from Omaha was accomplished without incident. Although the plan was to limit nighttime travel on the river above Omaha, the river channel here was well known for several miles, and by five A.M. the sky was ablaze, and Pruitt was having no trouble reading the river. Danny was patrolling the boat, from the engine room to the hurricane deck, making sure that the few passengers still awake were behaving themselves.

Three miles upstream from the *Clinton,* on a road that ran parallel to the river, Jack Galloway was leading three recruits on a hard ride to get ahead of his former employer. And also to get ahead of Harvey Blake, both physically and strategically. If Harvey Blake thought he had control of this operation, he had another think coming, in Galloway's mind. These three men would give him numerical superiority and let him take the lead once again.

Little Foot was a renegade Sioux who enjoyed violence and killing, particularly if it involved profit, although profit was not necessary. The main ingredient for a good time was bloodshed. He had no specific hatred for white men. He had found that Indian blood spilled as easily as white blood, and he made no distinction. He had two half brothers, Fred and Sam Walking Hawk, and they shared his love of violence. They were all armed with repeating rifles, as was Galloway. In addition, Galloway had a headdress and a breastplate to give him the appearance, at a distance, of a Sioux warrior.

Galloway had instructed these three desperadoes to shoot from the shore, targeting officers and Danny Barton. They were all able to swim. When the officers were dispatched, they would swim to the boat and make sure that Blake's methods of disabling the *Clinton* were working. He had some ideas of his own in that regard, and the end result would be the total destruction of the *Clinton* and the death of Harvey Blake.

Chapter Twenty-four

Harvey Blake was sitting in the main cabin, by himself, except for the number of men sleeping on the floor around him. Dink and Edward were down in the cargo bay. Blake watched as Danny walked slowly through the main cabin. He stopped and gave Blake a long look and then continued through the cabin. His next stop was the hurricane deck.

Blake got up and went to the exit facing the western shore. A mile ahead, he could see a column of smoke. The sun was just breaking the horizon in the east. He walked forward in the cabin until he thought he was exactly underneath the wheel stanchion in the pilothouse. The wheel was centered over the cabin, but the passageway where he stood, between the kitchen and the purser's office to the main stairway, was also centered and he could see no cables. The steering cables must be offset to one side, or perhaps they ran above the decorative ceiling between the hurricane deck and the main cabin. If the latter were the case, the cables would probably run the full length of the cabin and then turn down at the aft end of the ladies' portion of the main cabin. He walked down the center of the main cabin, stepping around snoring men while looking at the ceiling. Halfway through the length of the cabin, he saw a wooden plate screwed to the ceiling.

Blake stepped up onto a table but could not reach the ceiling. He picked up a chair by its back, lifted it onto the table, and stepped up on it. That gave him the height that he needed.

He had several tools in his pocket, one of which was a screw-driver. He removed the screws and found what he was looking for: two parallel cables, moving occasionally as Robert Pruitt, unaware of what was going on below him, maneuvered the *Clinton* in the sunrise.

Blake fished a clamp out of his pocket and quickly placed it on both cables, pulling them together. Pruitt made a course correction toward the eastern shore and held the *Clinton* in a slow turn to starboard. While the steering cables paused in their near-constant adjustment responding to Pruitt's movements at the wheel, Blake tightened the clamp. Pruitt's leverage at the wheel was enough to overcome the clamp, but just barely. Blake had anticipated this and quickly applied another clamp, and then another. He didn't take the time to replace the cover, but stepped down to the table and then to the floor, taking the chair and the wooden hatch cover with him. He dropped the cover on the seat of a chair next to the wall and went to the exit to assess the effect his work was having.

In the pilothouse, Pruitt watched the column of smoke on the shore with curiosity as the *Clinton* churned by. He began his correction to starboard and then felt the wheel stiffen. Thinking it was driftwood lodged in the rudders, he first rattled the wheel then he put his weight into it and managed to accomplish the correction he had started. But when he tried to bring the rudders back amidships, the wheel wouldn't budge. The *Clinton* was making a slow turn toward the eastern shore of the Missouri River. Unable to move the wheel in either direction, he rang the engine room for full stop. Then he pulled the cord for the steam whistle and didn't release it. The *Clinton* was in trouble.

Roustabouts, sleeping in various locations in the cargo bay, leaped to their feet and ran to the bow. Second mate David Erickson led the way. Pruitt stepped out of the pilothouse and yelled to the gathering crew. "Anchor over the bow! Now!"

While this was going on and all the crew, including the

stokers, were trying to puzzle out what was wrong, Dink walked by the larboard firebox and threw a log into it. He had hollowed the log and filled the space with black powder, then plugged the opening. In the glowing coals of the firebox it would be only minutes before the powder reached its ignition point.

A medium anchor was always kept at the ready. Four men lifted the anchor and threw it over the larboard bow. The heavy line snaked out, and the men snubbed the end to a cleat. The anchor skidded along the bottom, seeking a purchase, but it was too late. The *Clinton,* broadside in the stream and out of the channel, slid over a sandbar at her midships and the huge boat rocked ponderously to one side and then stopped.

Riverboats were not like ocean boats. They were lightly constructed, long and thin, made for flat, shallow water, and would flex in the small waves produced by a navigable river. A certain amount of this was tolerated, but in order to have at least some rigidity, bigger ones were often rigged with huge cables anchored at the bow and stern, and passing over stanchions above the hurricane deck. Even these cables were not enough if the boat were resting on an area in the middle with the ends supported only by water. Such was the case with the *Clinton.*

Erickson knew this and that the boat was in peril. "Get those hatches off the cargo hold and put the pump in gear!" he shouted. "We're gonna start making water!"

Dink and Edward, working as if they were ordinary roustabouts, removed a cargo hatch and Edward let himself down into the hold with an ax. His feet landed in two inches of water. It was difficult to swing the ax, as the cargo hold was less than six feet deep. When he swung the ax as effectively as he could, it just bounced off the seasoned timbers of the hull. He threw the ax into the cargo hold and pulled himself back onto the floor of the cargo bay.

"That ain't gonna work, Ed, but it don't make no difference. She's floodin' anyway."

"All right. Let's find Blake, get our money, and get out of here." The two of them ran out of the cargo bay.

Danny, hearing the constant whistle, ran across the hurricane deck to the pilothouse, nearly colliding with the captain as he did so. The captain followed him into the pilothouse where Robert Pruitt was examining the steering cables. They wound around the hub of the wheel. He had a pry bar that he was using to turn the spindle that held the steering cables, hoping he could dislodge what he still believed was driftwood in the rudders. He looked up as they came in.

"The rudders are jammed!" Pruitt said, getting to his feet.

"Very well, Mr. Pruitt. See to it." The captain did not want to take command away from his pilot.

"Yes, sir. We put an anchor out, but she ran aground before it could take hold. Erickson is pumping the hold in case we take on water."

Steve Allenby entered the pilothouse, tucking in his shirt. He had been sound asleep, off watch, and trying to make up for the sleep he had lost while the boilers were cleaned at Omaha. Charles Felden was right behind.

"Rudders are jammed!" Pruitt repeated. "We're pumping. Take a crew out in the yawl and reset the anchor as far upstream as you can get. We need to get off this sandbar before she breaks her back."

"You got it," Allenby said. He realized the urgency of the situation and ran from the pilothouse to the hurricane deck, followed closely by Charles Felden.

Chapter Twenty-five

The *Clinton* was grounded broadside with her stern facing the western shore. Jack Galloway and his three accomplices rode to a spot opposite the boat. They jumped off their horses and ran to the top of a grassy hill overlooking the river. From their position on the shore they could see the stern wheel and the hurricane deck, but because of the angle of the boat, the walkways along the sides of all three decks on the starboard side were out of their sight. But they could see a little of the larboard walkways. Only the top of the pilothouse was visible, and they had no opportunity to fire at the officers until Allenby came out onto the hurricane deck to supervise the lowering of the yawl.

Felden descended the stairs to take command of the yawl once it was in the water. Galloway's outlaw recruits began firing, but Allenby and one roustabout succeeded in lowering the yawl to the water before Allenby was hit in the chest. He collapsed on the hurricane deck. Two of the shots traveled the length of the boat and shattered the glass in one of the pilothouse windows.

Alerted by the broken window, Danny stepped out of the pilothouse, onto the walkway, and saw the men standing at the top of the bank, almost level with the hurricane deck, two hundred yards away. The morning sun made them stand out like Christmas tree ornaments. He brought his rifle up and began shooting rapid fire. He thought he hit one of the men; all four of them disappeared from his sight. He reloaded as he walked aft on the hurricane deck to get a closer shot should they reappear and to rescue Allenby. He heard several more shots, and a bullet splintered the cabin wall next to him, but he saw nothing. He quickened his step so that he might get a clearer view of the men on the bank. Not knowing Weedeater's exact location on the boat, he shouted out as loudly as he could for help.

"Weed! Come to the hurricane deck!"

Weedeater had been sleeping in a berth in the main cabin and rolled out of his bunk, rifle in hand. He pulled on his boots and ran to the cabin exit and toward the stairway up. Jimbo, being an ordinary roustabout, was sleeping in the cargo bay, and Weedeater didn't take time to fetch him.

It was then that the dynamite in the firebox exploded. It blew the door off the firebox and scattered embers in front of the box in the cargo bay and out onto the bow. It also dislodged the boilers and sprung the plates so that steam escaped in all directions. It caused considerable panic among the roustabouts; they had all heard nightmare stories of boilers exploding, but they didn't know which way to go to find safety. Many of them could not swim.

On the bow Erickson was almost knocked down by the force of the blast. Seeing the embers scattered all over the bow, it appeared to him as though the entire vessel was ablaze. He grabbed two roustabouts by their arms as they rushed by looking for safety somewhere in the confusion.

"Get some hose and start putting water on this fire!" He grabbed a retreating roustabout and turned him toward the hose. The others followed his command, and soon they were spraying the bow with water from the bilges.

The *Clinton* was not quite perpendicular to the stream. Anyone on the larboard side was at risk from the gunmen on the shore. Abigail's cabin was the last cabin on that side. As Danny rushed past with his rifle, she opened her door.

"What's happened, Danny?"

"Not sure, Miss Demille. Stay in your cabin. There are people shooting at the boat."

"Shooting!"

"Yes! Please stay in your cabin."

"Is anyone hurt?"

"Yes! Steve Allenby has been shot," he said over his shoulder as he gestured toward the yawl and Allenby's supine figure. "I'm going to try to get close enough to help him." At that remark, he spotted one of Galloway's men running in a crouched posture to find another shooting position on the bank. He raised his rifle and shot several times, levering a shell into the chamber after each shot. The man disappeared again. Danny kept his eyes on the bank as he reloaded the repeater.

Abigail came out of her cabin with her bag in her hand. She ran past Danny as he paused to shoot and headed directly for Allenby. Danny followed and, taking up a position in front of her and the motionless form, started shooting at anything that moved or looked out of place on the western shore.

On the cargo deck Erickson had had some success in preventing the fire from spreading to the cargo and the walls of the cargo bay until the pump failed due to the loss of steam. The doctor engine that powered the pump was in turn powered with steam from the larboard boilers. They were directly connected to each other and also to the starboard boilers by a pipe with a valve. When the larboard firebox exploded, the warped plates on the larboard boilers allowed steam to escape. For a few moments, it was replaced by steam from the starboard boilers, until they too began to run short of steam. The fireman was forced to isolate the starboard boilers to prevent the water remaining in them from flashing to steam. Then he began cooling the fires in the remaining firebox since the water in the boilers could not be replaced without the doctor engine. Without water, they would also warp from the heat of the firebox and ultimately fail. It might have been better to sacrifice the boilers to get the last bit of firefighting water onto the deck fires, but there was no one to make that decision, and his only responsibility was the boilers.

Erickson, not about to give up, organized a bucket brigade and began fighting a delaying action on the deck fires. His roustabouts were holding their own against the fires, but there was a new danger. Without the doctor engine to power the pumps, water began accumulating in the cargo hold. The weight of the water was pressing down on the bow and stern, springing the butts of the hull planks and increasing the leaks.

Peter Van Dusen, William Brown, and both firemen began dismantling the steam pipes to reconfigure them to supply the doctor engine from the starboard boiler. Cast iron holds heat for a long time, and it was hot, painful work. That kind of modification would ordinarily take half a day, with cool machinery. They knew they didn't have that long.

On the hurricane deck Abigail had slowed the bleeding from Allenby's wounds, and Danny was dragging him back toward the pilothouse and cover. The captain had been in front of the pilothouse observing the firefighting efforts on the bow. Once he determined that the efforts at fighting the fires were as much as could be done, he walked around the pilothouse, where he observed Danny and Abigail rescuing Allenby. A shot rang out from the shore and Danny went down on one knee and then stood up again, blood staining the leg of his pants. The captain stepped back into the pilothouse to address Pruitt.

"Mr. Pruitt, I'm taking command of the *Clinton*. Take your rifle and help Mr. Barton and Miss Demille."

Pruitt had no skill with firearms, but he picked up the rifle with a "Yes, sir," and stepped to the door of the pilothouse. He felt both relief and disappointment at being sent from the pilothouse; he wasn't sure he was up to the responsibility of rescuing the *Clinton* from a situation not of his making, but he didn't like giving up. Neither was he sure of defending her with a firearm, but he turned to his task. A bullet ripped into the steps of the pilothouse, and he involuntarily flinched back. Then, as if the close bullet strike caused him no real concern, he examined the rifle, worked the lever uncertainly to insert a cartridge into the chamber, stepped to the railing, and took aim at a figure on the shore. He fired, but missed, and the man on the shore fired back and also missed. Pruitt decided not to waste time shooting at something he couldn't hit anyway and ran to help Danny. More shots came from the shore, cutting grooves and ripping splinters in the wood along the wall of the first-class cabins.

Isaac came out of the Vermont cabin and picked up Danny's rifle. Danny, having difficulty staying on his feet, pulled himself to the open door of the captain's cabin in time to see Isaac on the walkway with his rifle.

"Give me the rifle, Isaac, and take cover in the pilothouse," he commanded. "Men on the shore are shooting at us!"

Isaac handed the rifle to Danny and ran to the pilothouse. Danny put maximum effort into standing, but his leg wouldn't support any weight at all, and he used the doorway for support as he returned fire. It was then that Pruitt arrived.

"Do you know how to shoot, Robert?" Danny asked through clenched teeth.

"Not very well, I'm afraid," Pruitt replied.

"Just aim at the shore and shoot as fast as you can. When your rifle's empty, grab Allenby's collar and drag him around to the front of the pilothouse."

Pruitt didn't answer. He levered a shell into the Henry rifle, peered around the door jamb, and began shooting at the men on the shore. Firing from the shore stopped until he emptied the rifle. At that point Weedeater arrived on the hurricane deck. He didn't bother shooting around the door jamb, but took up a position out in the open on the walkway. This allowed Danny a clear field of fire from his position in the doorway, and the two of them made life for the outlaws on the shore increasingly difficult. Little Foot was critically wounded, and Galloway, with a bullet in one leg, was hiding behind a tree, waiting for a chance to escape. Fred and Sam Walking Hawk had captured their horses and retreated beyond rifle range to reevaluate their strategy. The big steamer was helpless and an easy target; they just needed to concoct a plan to take advantage of her predicament.

Pruitt succeeded in dragging Allenby to the deck in front of the pilothouse, where Abigail could again tend to him without risk from the shore. The captain joined her.

"Abigail, there may be more injured men on the cargo deck," the captain said. "As soon as you do what you can for Mr. Allenby, they need you there. I'll try to find Eleanor and send her to help."

"How's Danny?"

"He appears to be shot in the left leg. He's holding his own."

"All right, Captain. This man has a bullet in his chest. He's dying and there's nothing more I can do." She stood up slowly. She had been in this type of situation many times and was realistic, but saddened.

"I'm sorry to hear that," the captain said, glancing around the pilothouse at the shore from which the gunfire had come. There was no forward stairway from the hurricane deck to the main salon. "Abigail, use the starboard staircase. The gunfire is coming from our left quarter. And go quickly." He left her and climbed the half stairs to the pilothouse to find Isaac there.

"Isaac, you'll be my runner. Use the starboard stairs." He pointed to make sure Isaac understood. "I'll be on top of the pilothouse."

Isaac had seen violence. He said nothing but looked up at the captain calmly, waiting for more instructions. The captain climbed to the roof of the pilothouse, in plain view of the hostile shore, and began appraising what he could see. He walked to the front of the pilothouse and looked down at Isaac, who was still waiting silently on the forward hurricane deck.

"Isaac, find Mr. Van Dusen. I want a report on damage. Find out. Go!" Isaac was off at a run.

The captain observed the efforts of Pruitt, Weedeater, and Danny at eliminating the threat from the shore. Muzzle flashes from the shore were few as the three kept up a steady rate of fire. Occasionally a bullet, with a clank, would strike the exhaust stack that towered over the pilothouse, but the captain paid the sounds no mind. At Danny's instruction, Pruitt returned to the captain's cabin for more ammunition. Culpepper turned his attention to the bow, where there were still numerous fires burning. The yawl, with three roustabouts, was close on the bow, the men maneuvering to keep the *Clinton* between themselves and the guns on the shore. The captain shouted down to them. "Start laying anchors upstream, you men. Use as much line as we have!"

One of the men in the yawl protested. "Captain, they're shooting at us!"

"They're shooting at everyone. Get those anchors out!" As the captain shouted this, a bullet ripped at his sleeve, missing his arm. He scarcely noticed. "Now!" Three men on the bow brought the anchor to the yawl and passed it over, with efforts fueled by adrenalin. With the anchor onboard, the men began rowing furiously against the current, paying the line out and hoping to minimize their time exposed to the hostile shore.

Harvey Blake knew that he had to get the nameplate off the pilothouse. Edward and Dink found him on the walkway outside the main cabin, and the three of them ran aft to the starboard stairway up, at the same time that Abigail was descending. She turned to retreat, but it was too late. Blake grabbed her by one ankle as she tried to return to the hurricane deck.

Chapter Twenty-six

In the engine room the engineers and firemen had completed their task of installing temporary pipe between the starboard boilers and the doctor engine. There was still enough steam in the starboard boilers to start the doctor engine, and they opened the valves. The first priority was to start refilling the starboard boilers, as the water level was below the lower try-cocks. The fireman knew that there had to be some water left or they wouldn't have had enough steam to start the doctor engine. He slowly opened the valve to admit water into the boilers, anxious that they not fill so fast as to quench the steam. At the same time, he had the stoker begin building the fire up to normal temperature. It was a risky operation, filling and firing simultaneously. If the fire impinged on the boiler where there was no water on the other side, the plates could warp or even fail.

The makeshift steamline had been put in place without gaskets; there hadn't been time to cut new ones. Brown and Van Dusen were going back over the fittings with wrenches in an attempt to slow the escape of steam. The cargo bay was filled with clouds of vapor, and the temperature was over one hundred twenty-five degrees.

Isaac stumbled through the foggy cargo bay until he found William Brown. He knew he was one of the officers by his uniform.

"Are you Mr. Van Dusen?" he asked.

"No, son," Brown answered quickly. "He's right here some-where. What do you need?" Brown grunted as he pulled on his long wrench.

"The captain wants a damage report," Isaac replied.

"Tell him"—Brown paused while he ran the past few min-utes through his mind—"tell him we've lost the larboard boil-ers. We've bypassed the doctor engine to the starboard boilers and it's working now. There is fire on the bow, no fire in the cargo bay, and we're taking on water at about four inches per hour. Go!"

Isaac turned and ran out of the cargo bay and up the main stairway, then around the main salon to the starboard stairway leading to the hurricane deck. He was just in time to see Harvey Blake drag Abigail down the stairs. Edward and Dink spotted him but he retreated to the front of the second deck where he climbed onto the railing, then jumped up and grabbed the toe board on the hurricane deck. Like a monkey, he pulled himself up, and when he had gained the hurricane deck in front of the pilothouse, he waved at the captain to get his attention.

"Yes, Isaac, give me your report."

"Some men have Miss Demille down there!" He pointed down.

The captain stiffened. "How many men?"

"Three, I think."

"Give me the rest of your report, Isaac," he said.

"But they're going to . . ."

"What did Mr. Van Dusen tell you?" the captain reiterated.

Isaac took a deep breath. "The larboard boilers are broke. The doctor engine is . . . uh . . ."

The captain, knowing every Detail of the boat's operation, anticipated the next statement. "Bypassed to the starboard boilers?"

"Yes, yes. And there is no fire in the cargo bay, and we're taking water at four inches per hour."

"Very good, Isaac. Get into the pilothouse and lock both doors until I knock three times on the roof."

"Yes, sir!" Isaac replied and wasted no time following the captain's instructions. Edward and Dink tried to catch him before he got into the pilothouse, but they were too late. Edward pointed his pistol through the glass at Isaac, but Isaac dove under the chart table. The captain observed all this from the roof of the pilothouse, but he was well back from the edge and was not seen by either outlaw.

"Come on, Dink," Edward said. "Let's find the safe. It ain't in there, and we don't need the kid." The two of them retreated down the starboard walkway in search of a cabin with a safe.

The captain leaned over the larboard railing and shouted to Pruitt, who was loading his rifle. "Mr. Pruitt! We have been boarded by outlaws. Miss Demille has been captured on the boiler deck. Take Mr. Koslosky and ensure her safety. Mr. Barton will hold this position." It was a battlefield, and Captain Culpepper was in command, as he had been during the Civil War.

Chapter Twenty-seven

Fred and Sam Walking Hawk were not ready to give up on a scheme that had promised so much. They tied their horses behind the hill and then descended into a gully that led to the water's edge.

"We could swim over, holding our pistols and powder above the water," Fred said.

"No. They'd spot us easy. We'd be like crows on a telegraph line. Let your Colt get wet," Sam countered. "It don't look like there's any shortage of guns on that there boat. We'll use our knives to get what we need."

At the water's edge, they slipped into the river, waded out into waist-deep water, and then began swimming across the two hundred yards that separated them from the *Clinton*. For a while they tried to swim directly to the boat, but then when they realized the current was taking them away, they tried to swim against the current.

Jimbo had been sleeping in the cargo bay when the firebox exploded. He escaped injury and, leaving his rifle behind, pitched in to control the fire. Then he heard the gunshots above the commotion of the firefighting efforts and handed his bucket to another roustabout. He retrieved his rifle and walked the lower walkway as far as the stern wheel, but his position was too low to see any of the outlaws on the top of the riverbank. He let himself into the engine room and crossed to the far exit on the larboard walkway. He couldn't figure out what was going on, or where he might help.

When he stepped out onto the walkway, he spotted the Walking Hawk brothers swimming toward the *Clinton*. Although they were both good swimmers, it takes an exceptional swimmer to swim faster than two miles per hour, and the current here was nearly twice that. They were losing ground, going downstream in spite of their best efforts. They realized that the channel was too much for them and changed course to swim to the downstream portion of the sandbar that had imprisoned the *Clinton*. Once they got their feet under them in knee-deep water, they began walking toward the boat. Jimbo watched as the exhausted pair struggled against the current flowing over the shifting sand, nearly half a mile away. He decided that this was where he needed to be. They were not going to board the *Clinton* if he could help it.

Blake hauled the struggling Abigail into the main salon where he found Skeet, who was trying to reassure the wakened passengers. Skeet pulled a gun from under the bar, but Blake leveled his own revolver at Skeet and then pointed it at Abigail's head.

"Toss that scattergun over the bar, bartender." He pulled the hammer back on his revolver to emphasize his command. Skeet had no choice. The shotgun would have been a poor weapon to use as long as Blake had Abigail in his grip.

"Where's the safe?" Blake demanded.

"In the captain's cabin," Skeet replied. Blake aimed at Skeet, but Skeet had been a bartender a long time and had been threatened at gunpoint before. He dropped behind the bar before Blake could pull the trigger. Blake cursed and then scooped up the shotgun as he pushed Abigail out the door. He threw the gun into the river and, holding both of Abigail's wrists in his

large fist, pushed her aft toward the stairway up to the Texas
deck.

Fern came from the kitchen in time to hear Skeet's response
to the question and to see Blake force Abigail ahead of himself, out the door. She realized that her baby and her friend
Isaac were in danger and ran out the other exit to find her baby
and protect him.

Edward and Dink ran aft on the walkway, around the bathhouse and forward on the larboard walkway of the Texas deck.
The first cabin was Abigail Demille's and the door was still
standing open. They glanced in and saw nothing other than
two single beds and a table.

Barton had lain down in the pilot's Iowa cabin in order to
stay out of sight of the shore. He would periodically sit up and
scan the shore, and then, seeing nothing, he would lay back
down to conserve his strength. Fred and Sam Walking Hawk
had abandoned the shoreline, Little Foot lay dying, and Galloway was hiding, just trying to survive. Barton had lost blood,
and, although he had tied a kerchief tightly around his wound
to stem the flow, he was becoming weaker.

The next cabin that Edward and Dink came to was the Vermont cabin. Isaac had been caring for Fern's baby there when
the shooting started. He had locked the door when he left. The
presence of a lock made Edward and Dink suspicious, and
they kicked the door in just as Fern reached the top of the
stairs, twenty feet from her cabin. She screamed and charged
the men before they had a chance to use their guns to defend
themselves.

The two men would have had an easier time putting a night-
gown on a mountain lion than fighting off Fern's wild attack.
Her baby was in danger, and she was screaming wordlessly as
she used her hands, feet, and teeth to defeat the two outlaws.
And she was winning. Fortunately for them, her screams at-

tracted Pruitt and Weedeater, who had been sent to rescue Abigail. In no time they had pulled Fern from the hapless pair and pushed them into Abigail's cabin and jammed the door. This all took place on the larboard side of the Texas deck.

Blake forced Abigail up the starboard stairs to the Texas deck and forward toward the pilothouse. He spotted the captain standing on top of the pilothouse and shouted to him to open his safe as he held his revolver to Abigail's head. The captain jumped down to the roof of the cabins and then to the platform at the door of the pilothouse. From there he walked toward Harvey Blake, fire in his eyes. It was bad enough for this band of cutthroats to threaten his vessel, but to put the life of the woman he admired in danger was more than he could take.

"Open your safe, old man, or I'll kill this woman!"

The captain made no reply but continued walking toward Blake. Blake suddenly realized that the captain's only intention was to deal with him, and he tried to level his revolver at the captain's head. Abigail's struggling prevented him from steadying his gun and his shot went wild. The captain strode purposefully toward Blake as Blake fired another wild shot. By then the captain was close enough for Blake to touch, but the look in the captain's eyes had taken his nerve. He dropped Abigail to use both hands on his revolver. The captain swung a fist and broke Blake's jaw. Blake recoiled, and the captain stepped forward again as Abigail fell out of his way. He used his other fist to hit Blake squarely in the nose, breaking his nose. Blood gushed from Blake's face; he cursed and raised his revolver with both hands. The captain brushed the revolver aside with his left hand and hit Blake one more time on the bridge of his nose. Blake fell, unconscious, to the deck.

Captain Culpepper picked Abigail up and wrapped his arms around her. The two of them stood there silently for a moment, and then the captain released her and lifted a loose strand of hair from her face. Pruitt and Weedeater came around the front of the pilothouse, drawn by Blake's wild shots, with guns at the ready. Fern, holding her baby tightly to her breast, was close enough behind Weedeater to wear his clothes.

"Captain Culpepper, we've got two of 'em locked in the Vermont cabin," Pruitt informed. "They're still armed, but they can't get out."

"Very well. Take this man and throw him in with the other two."

Abigail, in spite of the recent threat to her life, had kneeled down beside the injured Blake to assess his injuries. Now she stood up slowly. "This man is dead, Barnard."

"Throw him in with the other two anyway," was the captain's terse reply.

"Yes, sir," Weedeater said and grabbed Blake's lifeless hands, waiting for Pruitt to take his feet. Pruitt didn't move. He cleared his throat.

"Captain Culpepper?" he said.

"Yes, Mr. Pruitt."

"I'd like to take over command of my boat now."

Captain Culpepper looked at his son. He was standing straight and tall, a rifle in his hand and a calm strength in his voice. This young man, although skilled, had come aboard as a boy. He was now a man.

"All right, son, she's yours. Have Isaac let you into the pilothouse, and keep him around as a messenger."

"Yes, sir!" Pruitt said, and then added, "Thanks . . . Dad."

The captain turned to Abigail. "Abigail, there are many injured people onboard. Start with Mr. Barton." He pointed down the walkway to where Danny stood unsteady on his legs, a smoking rifle in his hand. At that moment the already damaged door to the Vermont cabin shattered and burst open. Edward and Dink came out with guns drawn.

Danny's rifle was empty, but his pistol wasn't. He dropped

the rifle and pulled his Colt from its holster as fast as he could; at a distance of forty feet, he shot Edward dead before Edward had a chance to cock his revolver. Dink retreated rapidly to the aft end of the Texas deck, turned, and shot once without aiming. Cocking his revolver, Dink shot again. Both shots missed while Danny calmly took aim and shot Dink dead.

"Are you all right, Mr. Barton?" the captain called.

Danny looked around at the group standing next to the pilothouse. Then he looked at his smoking pistol as his strength finally left him. Weedeater came to his side and caught him as he collapsed. Abigail was right behind Weedeater and immediately began working on Danny. It looked like the battle was over.

The captain addressed Fern. "Miss Fern, make your child comfortable in my cabin. Isaac is in the pilothouse, and he can help watch her. Find Eleanor and tell her Abigail needs help. She can come, or she can send someone."

"Yes, Captain. Thank you."

The captain faced Weedeater. "Mr. Koslosky, I'll help you take this body to the Vermont cabin now." The captain picked up the feet of the man he had just killed with his fists, and he and Weedeater carried him to the Vermont cabin.

Chapter Twenty-eight

As Pruitt leaned his rifle against the back wall of the pilot-house, David Erickson entered.

"The fires are all out. We've got two boilers, a hundred forty pounds of steam, the starboard engine on line, and the doctor engine is pumping the bilge."

"Is it keeping up?" Pruitt asked.

"Hard to tell. We're slowly turning to larboard; it's like she's pivoting on the sandbar. The bow is higher than it was, and the stern is lower. I've checked the number one hatch; the water is barely over the planks, but under the stern hatch, the water's eight inches deep. We may be holding our own, but I wouldn't even guarantee that."

"The wheel is turning now. Did you find out what happened to the rudders?"

"Yes. One of the outlaws clamped them together in the cableway above the main salon. We found the cover on the floor where he left it. If he had taken time to replace it, we'd still be looking."

"Good work. Where are the anchors?"

"There are two, both upstream from the bow."

"I'm going to gamble the leaks will slow down when she's fully afloat and on her lines again. Winch up hard on the anchors, and I'll start the engines in reverse. Be prepared to buoy the lines; we'll have to leave the anchors in the river if we get free. It takes too long to change from reverse to forward with just one engine."

"There's more current here than we've had before," Erickson reminded Pruitt. It would not be possible to continue their journey upstream with just two boilers and one engine.

"Yes, I know. We're going to turn and go back to Omaha. Perhaps we can get the larboard boilers repaired there."

"Very well, I'll see to the anchors," Erickson said and left the pilothouse.

Steamboats used two engines, out of phase by ninety degrees, so that one engine was always in position to power the paddlewheel over center. To start the paddlewheel with only one engine, the engineer had to turn the wheel with a long lever, a fraction of a degree at a time, until the one engine had a long push before the pitman arm centered, whether all the way forward or all the way to the rear. Then the inertia of the wheel would carry it over center. Pruitt rang for slow astern. After a delay so that the engineer could line up the pitman arm as described, the *Clinton*'s wheel began to turn backward. The deck crew used the powered capstan to slowly bring the anchor lines in, pulling the bow forward.

Fred and Sam Walking Hawk, under Jimbo's patient and watchful eyes, were almost to the *Clinton* when it started to slide backward off the sandbar and spin counterclockwise. They were afraid she would escape them, so they waded into deeper water to grab the low-riding footrail and pull themselves aboard. The water under the stern was barely deeper than the hull; the stern wheel in reverse created a forward flow, which helped them get through the deeper water without being swept downstream again. As the vessel spun around, they grabbed the footrail and hung on with all their remaining strength as the motion of the hull tried to tear them loose. Then the wheel was taken out of gear and the wheel brake was applied skillfully to stop the pitman

arm at the optimum position to start the wheel forward. In forward gear, the nearly drowned outlaws were overcome by the
movement of the water and had to release the foot rail. They
were sucked back under the hull and into the paddles, turning
only inches from the sandy bottom. Two of the most dangerous
men in the west perished, by accident, without a sound.

Jimbo walked from side to side of the *Clinton,* through the
engine room. He watched both sides of the river for any sign of
the men, but saw nothing and concluded correctly that they were
not as strong as the paddlewheel of the *Barnard Clinton.* He
shrugged and headed for the pilothouse to relate the story of the
two would-be boarders, and see where he might be needed next.

From the river, Jack Galloway had been able to see most of
the action onboard the *Clinton* and realized that the scheme had
collapsed. He watched as the big boat, unable to gain on the current with only one engine, began a turn into the main channel to
return to Omaha. Then he saw Captain Culpepper standing over
a kneeling woman and a prone man.

Abigail removed the bullet from Danny's leg and stitched
the hole closed. Then she put a dressing and a tight bandage on
it. "Danny, you just stay right here. I'll find help to carry you to
your cabin." As she talked, she pulled a carpet from the pilot's
cabin where Danny lay, rolled it up, and placed it under his leg.

The captain had been concerned about his wounded security
officer. Satisfied, he touched Abigail on the shoulder and walked
to the front of the hurricane deck, in front of the pilothouse. The
Clinton was now perpendicular to the flow and in midchannel.
She had just enough room to complete her turn downstream. Her
bow was now less than one hundred fifty yards from the western
shore.

Galloway was seething with anger at having been cheated
out of his prize. Nothing had gone right for him since leaving
the *Clinton.* He had hoped in vain that Fred and Sam Walking
Hawk would be able to board the *Clinton*, but they had appar-

ently been killed by the very boat they had tried to victimize. It would have been a much easier task than before to swim to the *Clinton* where she now was, but he didn't have the strength to try it because of his wound. But as the bow of the *Clinton* floated past, he saw the captain in front of pilothouse, within easy rifle range. He picked up his rifle, steadied himself against the tree he had been using for cover, took careful aim, and pulled the trigger. The bullet struck the captain in his collarbone on his left side, breaking the bone and taking his breath away. Abigail cried out as he collapsed on the deck.

Danny sat up as the captain fell, and the sound of the shot reached the boat. He could clearly see Galloway on the grassy hill standing next to a small tree. Although the position of his body was awkward, he leveled his rifle with one arm and fired. Bark flew off the tree next to Galloway's face. He awkwardly worked the lever and shot again, and again, and again, until the turning of the *Clinton* robbed him of his field of view.

Jimbo had just come up to the Texas deck on the starboard side. He had an unobstructed view of Galloway holding the rifle, and he began shooting. Galloway would have retreated, but two of Danny's shots had hit him and he was holding to the tree to keep from falling. This made a good target for Jimbo, and he finished what Danny started. When he saw Galloway fall, he ceased his shooting and walked around the pilothouse to the larboard deck.

"Jimbo!" Abigail said loudly but calmly. "Send Eleanor to me." She began unbuttoning the captain's coat. Danny, watching from his reclining position, opened her bag for her and pushed it to her side.

"Thanks," Abigail said in a low voice. She used a knife to cut away the captain's coat and shirt, revealing a hole in his left front shoulder and a larger hole in his back, right through his shoulder blade where the bullet exited. The back of his shirt was heavy with blood.

Jimbo returned in minutes with Eleanor right behind him. Abigail glanced up at the shoreline. The *Clinton* had completed her turn and was heading downstream. "Are we returning to Omaha?" she asked.

"Yes, ma'am," Jimbo answered. "It sure looks like it."

"Find out from the pilot how long before we get there. We need a hospital for the captain!"

Jimbo ran the short distance to the pilothouse. He was back in seconds. "Mr. Pruitt says we'll be opposite Omaha in two or three hours, but it'll take us awhile to tie up there because we have only one engine."

"Mercy!" Abigail cried. "All right, I'm going to operate right here on the boardwalk. Eleanor, I need several basins of hot water. See that they are brought here, but don't wait for them to be prepared. I need you right here."

"Yes, ma'am," Eleanor replied and left quickly.

Danny rolled over on one side so he could see Abigail. "Miss DeMille," he asked, "did I hear you say you were going to operate?"

"Yes, Danny. And it's actually Doctor DeMille."

"You're a doctor?"

"Yes, a surgeon."

"Does the captain know?"

"I started to tell him once, but we were interrupted. He'll know if . . . when he wakes up."

"What are you going to do?" Danny asked.

"First, I've got to stop the bleeding. Then I'll have to see if I can save his arm."

"Is there anything I can do to help?"

"Yes, lie still and be quiet so that I don't have to attend to you while I'm working on Barnard."

Danny didn't reply; he laid back down in the doorway to the Iowa cabin.

Eleanor returned and said, "They's boilin' water for you now, Miss DeMille. It'll be here directly."

Abigail used the washbasin in the captain's cabin to wash her hands. She found fresh linens in his closet and spread them on the deck where he lay, and then she told Eleanor to wash her hands also. She opened her case and laid out her instruments.

"Can you count, Eleanor?" she asked.

Eleanor was slightly offended. "'Course I can."

Abigail smiled slightly and briefly at the irony in Eleanor's voice, but she was all business. "I'm laying out these instruments, and we'll give them each a number according to how far they are from *me*. If I ask you for number seven, which one would you pick up and hand me?"

Eleanor pointed impatiently to a bistoury, the seventh tool in line from Abigail.

"Good, let's get started. Number two, please." Eleanor picked up a scalpel and handed it to Abigail, who began exposing the damaged flesh in Captain Culpepper's shoulder.

Robert Pruitt was aware of the plight of his father, but there was little he could do. The *Clinton* was headed downstream with half power, taking on water, and missing several crew members. Even when he got off watch, someone would have to fill in for the first mate, Steve Allenby, who was lying dead in his cabin. He himself would have to share Allenby's duties with David Erickson, the B-watch mate.

Getting to the wharf at Omaha would be more difficult without full power. He was thinking about possible solutions to this problem when Charles Felden came to the pilothouse. It was twenty minutes until eight in the morning.

"Robert," Felden said, "we have six and a half inches of water in the hold. It's gaining at the rate of one inch per hour at full pump capacity."

"Most of our freight is eight inches off the planking, right?"

"Yes."

The bare hull of the *Clinton* could hold about five thousand gallons of water per inch. Pruitt's concern was not for the freight in the hold, but that when the water reached the freight, because of the space that the freight occupied, the water level would rise much faster in the hull at the same rate of leakage. And as the hull sank lower in the water, the water pressure against every leak would increase. If that weren't enough, because of the extra weight, the vessel would respond slowly to changes in direction and increases in power.

"It's going to be close, isn't it?"

"I'm afraid so. We've managed to run a steam pipe from the starboard boilers to the fixed cutoff valve on the larboard engine."

"That can give us a burst of power, but we have only two boilers. We run the risk of losing steam."

"Yes. We can get one burst of full power; Van Dusen estimates twenty seconds' worth. And then we'll have less than half power for many minutes."

"Well, Charles, you'll be on the wheel when we reach Omaha. Where do you want me?"

"In the engine room. I don't have a mate. We'll continue to use the lad as a messenger." Felden nodded at Isaac who was in the pilothouse, awaiting instructions. "Do you have any ideas on docking?"

"Yes. If it were me on watch, I'd put the yawl out with as much heavy line as we have. We'll have to turn upstream to pull into the wharf. Six good oarsmen can make more headway into the current than the *Clinton*." Felden was already nodding. It was the same scheme he would have used. Pruitt was thinking well. They would try to get a line ashore and then use the doctor engine to pull the *Clinton* into its berth.

When Felden took over the watch minutes later, Pruitt went

to the main deck and organized a crew to man the yawl. They coiled the heavy line into the bottom of the yawl and waited, watching downstream for the river town of Omaha.

When the Omaha wharf was in sight, Felden put the *Clinton* into a tight turn. He drifted down toward Omaha, stern first, the wheel at low speed, conserving steam. The yawl was in position at the bow, the end of the coiled line made fast to the bow of the *Clinton*, and six of the best oarsmen onboard.

Long before the *Clinton* had Omaha in sight, Doctor DeMille had done all she could do for Captain Culpepper. His shoulder was a collection of bone chips, silver wire, and silk thread, and it was covered in heavy bandages in an attempt to keep it immobile. A person's right lung has three lobes; the left has only two. It was fortunate that he had been shot in the left side, where only forty percent of his lungs were in peril, but any injury to either lung was potentially lethal. Abigail could only hope that the injured lung would keep working, and so far it had. With help from the crew, she had modified his bed so that he would rest in a semi-reclining position. She was now most interested in how long it would be before they arrived in Omaha. She doubted that there was any medical help in Omaha that could improve on what she had done, but she wanted the captain to be off the boat and in a hospital.

Abigail tapped lightly on the open door of the pilothouse. Without looking to see who was there, Felden said, "Yes?"

Steamboats are designed to go forward, not backward. Felden had posted a lookout on the hurricane deck, looking over the paddlewheel to watch for hazards. Felden could look over the tops of the staterooms and see the man's head and his arms if he raised them. He could also step out of the pilothouse on either side and see if something was approaching from the leading rear quarter. There was no reason to look out the forward windows as everything in view from there was receding.

"Mr. Felden, I have treated the captain. He is doing poorly and needs to be in a hospital and receive constant nursing as soon as possible." She only wanted him to know the situation and turned to go as soon as she had given the information.

"Miss DeMille?"

She paused and waited as he craned his neck to check the lookout, looked out both sides, and then moved the wheel only a little. He looked out both sides of the pilothouse once more and then said, "What did your treatment entail?" He knew she had been useful in treating injuries onboard the *Clinton* and was already suspicious that she was more than just a compassionate person.

"Mr. Felden, for my own reasons, I have not been forthcoming about myself. I . . ." He held up his hand for her to be silent for a moment. The lookout on the hurricane deck signaled for a hard turn to starboard. A steam ferry that had been coming up along the eastern shore had turned to make the crossing behind the *Clinton* to Omaha, unaware that the *Clinton* didn't have enough power to go forward. Felden pulled long on the steam whistle to let the other vessel know she was in peril.

The lookout had correctly estimated that a turn to starboard would allow the other vessel just enough room to cross the channel before the *Clinton* drifted down on her. To turn the stern to starboard, Felden had to spin the wheel to larboard and the water moving over the rudders pushed the bow left and the stern right. He waited only a few seconds and, when he could see that the ferry was clear, he spun the wheel the other way.

"I can see you're busy, Mr. Felden. I just wanted to let you know."

"Thank you," he said, still watching the rearward progress of the *Clinton* and the lookout on the hurricane deck. "Tell me, is it Nurse DeMille, or Doctor DeMille?"

Abigail allowed herself a quick, discreet smile at his perception. She answered, "Doctor DeMille," and touched him on the arm as she left the pilothouse. She returned to the captain's cabin, where she sat by his side with Eleanor.

Felden opened the forward window in the pilothouse and shouted for the yawl to cast off and pull for the wharf. He rang for half speed from the engine room, and the wheel began to churn, but the *Clinton* still was going downstream, albeit more slowly than before. There was a space of about five boat widths that Felden decided was his best opportunity to safely berth the steamer. He pulled the steam whistle four quick pulls to indicate to the men in the yawl that they were just opposite his intended berth, and then he rang for full speed. The yawl, commanded by Robert Pruitt, cast off from the bow of the *Clinton*, paying out the heavy line.

The berthing scheme agreed upon by Felden and Pruitt worked perfectly. The men in the yawl reached the wharf and quickly tied off their heavy line and pulled the yawl out of the way. Then they signaled to the *Clinton* to take up the line, and the doctor engine began assisting the paddlewheel in moving the big sternwheeler to her berth. As the bow of the *Clinton* approached the landing at Omaha, Felden let the momentum of the vessel drive the bow into the mud. Pruitt had already left his crew in the yawl to run to town to fetch the doctor. At his instruction, one of the roustabouts in his crew found the wharfmaster and arranged for a second pump to help the *Clinton* stay ahead of her many leaks. In minutes, the *Clinton* was tied securely to the banks at Omaha and with the help of an additional pump, which was brought aboard in a freight wagon, was slowly gaining on the water in her hold.

Chapter Twenty-nine

Captain Culpepper remained unconscious or delirious for several days. At Felden's urging, Pruitt took over the captain's job. The *Clinton* wasn't going anywhere.

Pruitt contracted with several other steamers to deliver the Army freight to Fort Benton. It still allowed a small profit for the *Clinton*. Passengers who had booked to towns farther upriver were likewise transferred to other means of transportation. Some decided they had had enough of river travel and started out across the prairie in purchased wagons, on horseback, or even on foot. Pruitt kept a small crew of roustabouts to assist with repairs, but released the majority of the others. This crew was able to effect enough repairs to the hull to allow the *Clinton*'s pump to keep the hold dry, but there was still the matter of the boilers.

One of the two boilers was leaking in only a few places and was patched with wedges. The other was finally designated as scrap after many attempts at repair. The search for a replacement boiler had not produced any results so far. Pruitt and Felden sat at a table in the nearly deserted main salon and talked the matter over. In dealing with the various problems that beset the *Clinton*, the two had become close.

"The wharfmaster has offered to lease the *Clinton* through the winter as a wharf boat," Pruitt said.

"I guess you'll have to let the officers go," Felden said. "Too bad. It might be hard to come up with a crew this competent again. Even our roustabouts are pretty good men, better than you'll find in most river towns."

"I know. It seems a shame, but even if we go back to St. Louis, and even if there were a boiler available there, we wouldn't be able to make another trip this year. I can make full payroll only one more month without going into my father's savings."

"Well, it's your decision, Robert. I know it's not an easy one."

Doctor DeMille came into the salon at that moment. "Robert," she said, "your father is awake and is asking for you."

Pruitt stood up. "Maybe it won't be my decision after all," he said, and then followed Abigail to the wharf, where they hired a hack to take them to the hospital where his father had lain for four days. When they got there he was asleep again.

"Did he say anything, Miss . . . Doctor Demille?" Pruitt asked.

"He asked about the *Clinton,* I told him what I knew, asked him a few questions about how he felt, and then I left to find you."

Pruitt told Abigail in as few words as possible what the condition of the boat was and what he was doing. "I keep telling myself that he will recover and approve of what I've done."

"I'm sure that will be the case, Robert," Abigail said.

"I also tell myself that he is very fortunate that you are"—he paused as he looked for an appropriate word—"close."

The captain moaned once while Pruitt was talking. Abigail moved to his side. The two of them were silent for long moments, and then Pruitt spoke.

"How did you come to be here, Doctor DeMille?" Like his father, Pruitt would not have asked such a question in ordinary circumstance, but he felt that the two of them, because of their mutual concern for the captain, could talk frankly.

"I had a modest practice before the war. When the war started, I went to work in a hospital. I fell out of favor with the Army and eventually decided to find new surroundings."

Pruitt wanted to know more, but at that moment the captain took several deep, rasping breaths and then lay still. Abigail quickly leaned over to listen to his chest and then sat back down.

"He's not getting stronger. His breathing is more shallow, and his heart rate is rapid. He can't get stronger if he doesn't eat, and he can't eat until he gets stronger." Her eyes didn't meet Pruitt's as she slumped in the chair at the bedside, one hand on the captain's forearm. Her eyelids drooped, and then her eyes closed. Pruitt quietly left the room.

Weedeater's wounded arm prevented him from helping with the repairs on the *Clinton*. Fern took over as his nurse and she, her baby, and Isaac were never far from his side. He was given a small bonus by Pruitt for his valorous service during the attack. This was enough for him to buy a small plot of land upriver from Omaha, but he stayed on the *Clinton*, patrolling the decks with one arm in a sling and the other carrying his rifle.

Danny formed a rapport with Rake Angleton, the town marshal in Omaha. Angleton offered him a job when his work on the *Clinton* was done, but Danny had left a special person in Montana and was going to try to find another steamer going upriver, as soon as the *Clinton* was no longer in need of him. He, also, patrolled the decks, on crutches, a pistol at his side, while his leg healed.

A few passengers stayed onboard the *Clinton;* it was cheaper than a hotel in Omaha. Skeet could see no reason to put them off while there was still food and drink onboard. He even replenished some of the supplies so that, in the end, he would use all the stores up at the same time.

The kitchen, under Eleanor's supervision, continued to make

meals for a few workers and the passengers who stayed onboard. With the exception of Charles Felden, the officers all found employment on other vessels. To a man, they expressed regret at leaving and asked to be notified if the captain recovered and secured another boat, or, less likely, managed to restore the *Clinton*.

Van Dusen, the last to leave, came to the pilothouse in uniform, carrying a large duffel. "Mr. Pruitt?"

Pruitt looked up from some papers he was studying. "Yes, Peter. You're leaving now?" It was more a statement than a question.

Van Dusen set the suitcase down and stepped in to the pilothouse. "Is there any likelihood of putting the *Clinton* in service again?"

"That issue is in doubt. As you know, we've repaired all the leaks, but they may not hold if we put her into the river again. There's a boiler available from a maker on the Ohio, but I'm waiting to see what my father wants to do."

"The Old Man. Has he made any progress?" It was the most compassionate thing that Pruitt had ever heard Van Dusen say.

"No. He's been conscious several times, but gets weaker every day. He's too sick to live, and too stubborn to die." Pruitt didn't say it to be funny; it was an accurate description of the old warrior.

"I hope he makes it, Robert."

"Thanks, Peter."

"And I'll have to say that you're a pilot I'd serve with again, if the opportunity should come." Pruitt and Van Dusen shook hands, and then he was gone.

Several days later Pruitt gathered up papers and found Charles Felden. "Charles, I'm going into town to send telegrams to some investors who expressed interest in the *Clinton*."

"Are you going to the hospital?"

"Yes. Doctor Demille didn't come here last evening as she usually does. That makes me anxious. There has been nothing encouraging since his arrival in the hospital." Abigail had been giving them daily reports on the captain, and each day brought worse news. He was almost never conscious. He had a fever, periods of delirium, and had drunk very little and eaten nothing.

"Tell Miss DeMille not to give up on him. He's got strength we can't see."

Pruitt had to smile a little. "I don't think her giving up will be a problem." Then he was serious again. "She'll take it very hard if he doesn't make it, and it won't be because of her profession."

"That's an accurate statement, Robert."

"There'll be an appraiser here this afternoon. If I'm not back, show him around."

"Certainly."

Pruitt donned his officer's cap and left the pilothouse. Danny Barton met him on the bow.

"Are you going to visit your father, Robert?" he asked.

"Yes, and the bank and the telegraph office."

"Mind if I go with you?"

"No, of course not." Pruitt looked at Danny's crutches. "Let's find a hack."

The two men climbed into a hack at the wharf and settled in for the ride into downtown Omaha.

"What are your plans, Robert?" Danny asked.

"It depends on my father. I'm not a businessman. I'm just a river pilot, and one with limited experience, at that. But that's all I want to do. I'd like to be on the *Clinton* if she can be brought up to operating condition, or, if not, there are other good boats."

Danny watched Pruitt's eyes as he made this statement and thought he looked ten years older than he had the day he came onboard, just a few months ago. The youthful exuberance in his voice was gone, his eyes looked serious, and the strain of worrying about his father as he tried to conduct the business of a steamboat came through in every word he spoke.

"It's a good job," Danny stated the obvious.

"How about you, Danny? What are your plans?"

"I have a girl, three horses, and forty-three cows in Montana. We couldn't afford to get married, so I signed on for this trip on the *Clinton* while she stayed with friends, grazing the cows on their pasture. Since we didn't finish our trip, my payoff won't be enough to buy grasslands or build a house, but I'm not going to wait any longer. We'll have to live in a tent and graze free range for a while, but we'll make it."

"When you get ready to leave, let me know what you need, and I'll sign the check."

"I couldn't let you do that," Danny protested.

"I won't let you talk me out of it," Robert said firmly. "All this responsibility means I get to make the decisions. Some not so pleasant, some very pleasant. This is the latter. Consider it done."

Danny thought Pruitt was beginning to sound like his father, the captain. "I'll pay you back."

"Here's the hospital," Robert observed, closing the subject of Danny's final check.

When the two men walked into the hospital, they were assaulted by the smell of stale food, urine, and bodies in need of bathing. The front room in the hospital was small and bare except for five wooden chairs and a small table where a nurse sat talking to Abigail, who was writing something. She looked up as they walked in.

"Robert, Danny, I was just writing a note to send for you. Follow me." She wadded the note she had been writing and walked down the hall without waiting for them. They looked at each other and silently exchanged the opinion that there could only be bad news waiting for them. In spite of the dread they felt, they hurried after her.

In the hallway, the smells were more intense, and Danny wondered how a person could get well where the air carried nothing of the outside smells that he was so used to and relished. Near the end of the hallway, Abigail stopped at a door, opened it, and then stepped aside, smiling. As Danny and Robert entered, they saw Captain Culpepper, propped up on pillows, looking pale, but with his eyes wide and bright.

"Gentlemen, it's good to see you."